SUBSCRIBE

Text Shan to 22828 to stay up to date with new releases, sneak peeks, contest, and more....

THE WAY TO A KILLER'S HEART

NIECY P.

SHAN PRESENTS, LLC

THE WAY TO A KILLER'S HEART

Published by Shan Presents
www.shanpresents.com

WANT TO JOIN SHAN PRESENTS?

To submit your manuscript to Shan Presents, please send the first
three chapters and synopsis to submissions@shanpresents.com

ONE

JASON

Now fire when ready stay watchin now figure, increase speed,
  Make you muthafuckers bleed from your mouth quicker,
  Plus, all the niggas that you run with, be on some dumb shit,
  Trick on them hoes I ain't the one bitch

I HAD that Pac blaring through my system while I was driving to my next hit. Yeah muthafuckers, you heard that right. I was on my way to these noncompliant assholes that couldn't follow simple instructions. Don't come in our territory, selling new shit without introducing it to The Stand.

The Stand was a group of leaders that was over set territories. If there was anything new about what needed to be done, we would have a meeting to discuss this new shit and how it would benefit us all. Selfish muthafuckers didn't care about involving us. So, they sent me.

Who am I, you ask? Well, my name is Jason Davis. I am the second oldest and the most unstable Davis out here. I know I ain't right. So, does my oldest brother Jordan. He sent me because he knew that nobody would survive this massacre.

I joined the Navy when I was eighteen. I then enlisted in the Special Op training and became a Seal. I have been with that team for seven years. After my five-year mark, my mom begged me to come home. I know she missed me, but I wasn't returning the same way I left. I was in a dark place right now. I have been back home for almost six months, and I have not seen my mother yet. My mom was my light. Only she can bring me out of that darkness that drenches me. I didn't want to disappoint her, so I stayed away to put these assholes back in line.

I pulled up to the restaurant where these duck ass niggas were hanging out at. I lowered my music and cut the lights off my black on black Escalade. I loaded my two-custom made Berettas, pulled out my hunting knife, and three other smaller ones. My brother wanted a statement to be made, so I guess I'll be getting real dirty tonight. I got out my SUV and walked towards the back of the restaurant. When I got to the back, there were two guys standing by the door. Two silent kills. I rushed the one whose back was towards me, grabbed him by his throat, and threw a knife in the neck of the other. The other guy started struggling in my arm. Not wasting any time, I put my hands on his face and snapped his neck. I laid him on the ground and went to retrieve my knife.

I went into the door that they were guarding. I heard the men talking and laughing about some bullshit that was going on, on the big screen television that was over the bar. *Six of them, this shit should be a breeze.* I took out my guns and started shooting them while they were distracted. None of them had time to react or pull their gun out. I shot their leader Goose in the shoulder. Everyone else was shot in the head. I walked, stood over Goose, and he started begging for his life. I hated shit like this. Don't start begging now muthafucker. Take this shit like a man. But, I don't say anything. I usually don't. If I showed up on your doorstep, you pretty much knew that it was over for you. Bruh, the shit was so funny how this nigga was begging like Robin Thicke in this bitch.

"Come on, Jason, please let me talk to Jordan so we can get this shit straight. I'll give him all the money that we made through the month, man. Please Jason."

I took out my hunting knife and started thinking of the many ways I can slice his ass up. All the others didn't really have to suffer like him. Goose knew better, but I guess greed got the best of him. Oh well, judgment was already made.

"Wait, Jason! If you're going to kill me, please use the gun, man. Just kill me." He started making suggestions and shit. I stared down at him and wondered what his insides looked like. I fed off the fear in his eyes. I kneeled next to him and pushed the knife into his chest slowly. I knew the people in the neighborhood heard this fool screaming for his life, but I didn't care. When the knife was completely in, I dragged it all the way down to his dick. All his insides were spilling out his stomach. His cries became silent and I became bored. I wiped my knife on his shirt and walked to the bathroom to clean up. I walked out the back door and got into my truck to call my brother.

"It's done." I told him and hung up. My next call was to this bitch I fucked after nights like this. My adrenaline stayed up and I needed to calm it down before I started killing just because. "Where are you?"

"I'm at home," she said to me, trying to sound all sexy.

"Be ready, I'm on my way." I hung up after giving her my orders. She knew what that meant. Ass up, face down. I didn't need to see her face. I didn't want to. I cruise down the streets still blasting my Pac. I knew my mother was about to tell my pops about not seeing her. Hell, I haven't seen none of my family. Like I told y'all. I was fucked up. I couldn't let my family see me like this. It didn't have anything to do with me being ashamed. I just wasn't ready.

I pulled up to her house and jumped out. The door was unlocked, so I walked in and started getting undressed. Before letting my pants drop, I pulled the gold wrapper out. I went into her bedroom and saw nothing but ass. I stared at her glistening pussy while putting the condom on. Wasting no time, I grabbed my dick and slammed it into that wet shit. "Oh shit, Jason!" She screamed out while putting her hand back to slow my strokes down. I grabbed her arm, twisted it, and placed it on her back.

"Ahh!" Her screams became muffled by the pillows I stuck her head in. I fucked the shit out her. I was going deeper with every stroke. I let her hand go and grabbed her hair. She started screaming and moaning. The shit was turning me on even more. I wanted to cause her that type of pain that she liked. She stayed begging me to wrap my hands around her throat or to bite on her nipples. I was with it only if that was the type of shit she liked. I felt her pussy tightening up and knew that she was about to bust on my shit. I didn't slow down after her trembles subdued from her cumming. I went even deeper and harder. I was trying to hit that hoe fallopian tubes. Her ass was jiggling with each stroke. I slapped her on the ass and watched my handprint appear.

I pulled out and grabbed her arm to place her on the wall. She bent down and touched her toes. I pushed her back into the wall so that she was locked in that position. I placed my hands on the wall while my dick guided itself back in. She was trying to get loose, but it wasn't happening. I pulled out to the tip and slammed back in that shit. I felt my nut coming so I pulled out; she stood and kneeled to her knees. I pulled the condom off as she sucked the life out of my shit. My head went back, and I stared at the ceiling. Not satisfied at all, I was ready to go home. I pulled my dick out of her mouth and walked out her bedroom. I threw away the condom and gathered my clothes.

"Jason, why don't you stay the night? I can cook you breakfast in the morning and we can get to know each other." She said to my back.

I turned to face her, seeing her face for the second time. She was a beautiful woman, don't get me wrong. She was a dark skin chick with ass and thighs. She had a slender face and some cute ass lips. All in all, she couldn't fuck with me, though. I would ruin her mind, body, and soul. I continued putting my clothes on and grabbed my keys off the floor.

"No." I told her flat out with no room for discussion. I walked out, jumped my truck, and drove home with the radio off this time.

TWO

JORDAN

"It's done."

I heard him say before the beep. That was all I needed to hear. All I was going to hear. Jason was a man of few words. He was the type to let his actions speak for him. That's why he was one of the deadliest assassins out there. He was right up there with the Elites.

The Elites were a group of assassins that was run by Callum Bailey. Whenever a hit needed to be done, a call was made to Callum. He would send out Shadow, Death, or that crazy muthafucker Gage. They killed with no remorse whatsoever. My brother was like that as well. That's why I didn't need to call for the Elites.

I was in the office of my parents' home. My father had just stepped down and announced me as the leader of the Davis crew at the age of twenty-six. Jordan Davis is my name. Me and Joseph ran the operation with an iron fist. Joseph was the baby brother of the group at twenty-two, Jason was twenty-three. Anytime someone got out of line, I would send Jason. His ass didn't tolerate shit. He didn't come to any of the meetings we had with the Stand. He left that to us.

I was rearranging some papers on the desk when my father walked in with Joseph behind him. We all resembled both of our parents. Joseph was dark complexion, while Jason had a cocoa complexion. Joseph's hair was in a curly fade. Jason kept his in a low cut. Joseph was on the slim side at 6'5, and Jason was on the medium built at 6'6. The only thing that they had in common was their eyes, which was hazel, like my mother.

I was 6'6 like Jason and dark complexion like Joseph. I also kept my hair low with a little on the top. My mother told us that our faces were strong and defined like our father. She said it was scary sometimes of how much we looked alike. My father came and sat in front the desk. JJ went to the bar to get them cigars.

"Where is Jason?" My pops asked.

"He just finished the hit on the Tucks. He called to let me know it was done and probably went home." I told them. I really didn't know much about where Jason went after that.

"Find him and bring my boy home. His mother is very upset because he hasn't been by to see her yet. We know how Jason can get, but it is no excuse for him to not see your mother. Make it happen," my father said while lighting up his cigar.

I loved the smell of that shit. I couldn't smoke them though. I tried and failed miserably. That was a habit that my father shared with Joseph. Our habit was drinking. Crown or Cognac was our shared drink. We really didn't know what he did with Jason. They rarely got together. Jason was more of a momma's boy. I know. You can't tell from how he distanced himself from her.

My mother was his weak spot. Shit, she was all our weak spot, but Jason would go crazy if mother was harmed in any way. I called him and put it on speaker phone. His phone went straight to voicemail. "Mom." I said after the beep. He would know what that message meant.

"What else is going on with the Stand. Any news on the disappearance of Derrick's men." Joseph asked in his deep voice. We were trying to figure out why there was a hit on one of my dad's best friend. Derrick was on the Stand as well. His son, Drake, was missing along with some of the other men. He was supposed to take over the same time as me.

"I found out that Derrick owed a lot of money to the Mitchell family in Texas. They sent Geneva's assassins to complete the task. When Derrick didn't come up with the money, they started sending pieces of Derrick's oldest son, DJ to his house. His mother opened the box with his ring finger in it. I was going to send Jason to take care of that." I told them.

My father was shaking his head. "No, don't send Jason. Give him a break from all this shit. Call for one of the Elites. Put in an order for Gage to pay them a visit."

"Alright Pops. I'll get right to it." I replied to him. We sat and talked throughout the night about business and other random shit. It was about one in the morning when Jason walked in. He stood in the doorway for a minute before walking all the way in. My father got up and met him halfway. He grabbed Jason's face and stared. "Where is my boy?" He asked him.

"He's coming Pops." Jason told him.

My father smiled. He was looking for any damages that would have fucked Jason up mentally. Jason being Jason didn't show it though. But, what he did give my father was a glimpse of the little boy that used to sit under his desk during his meetings. My father pulled him into a tight embrace. My brother was not the one to show affection. But he held onto Pops like he didn't want to let go. Me and JJ walked up to them.

Pops pulled back. "Welcome home, son. You were missed."

"I missed you guys as well," he said. He walked past my father to us. JJ held out his hand and gave him a half-hug.

"Welcome home, big brother. You good?" JJ asked him. We all were worried about his state of mind. He was already jacked up before he left. The military just enhanced that shit by teaching him other ways to kill and get away with it.

"I'm good JJ. Jo, I'm good. I just need to get some rest. Other than that, I'm good," he told us. JJ looked back at me and I thought the same thing. He wasn't good, but he was done with the conversation.

"Yeah and a shave." JJ said to him. I took Jason's outstretched hand and pulled him into a hug like father did. JJ and Jason have always had that connection between them. They could feel each other's emotions and shit. Jason found a way to shut that shit down. He told JJ that he didn't want him to feel what he felt throughout the years. But, they remained close. I, on the other hand, didn't have a clue of what my little brother was going through and that shit killed me.

"I really missed you man. You shouldn't stay away that long." I pulled back from him.

He smirked at me. "Fuck, I'll miss me too, if muthafuckers around here not getting the job done. You been putting weak ass niggas on the payroll." He said with a full smile. Another thing we rarely see.

"So, I guess the old lady want to see me." Jason joked, but was serious

We all laughed at that.

My mom would curse his ass out if she would have heard him. "She is upstairs. Go see her son and put that smile on her face." Pops told him. He turned and walked out. My mother loved her some Jason. He was the most troubling one of the three. It didn't bother me and JJ at all. We knew that our mother loved us all, but Jason needed her more. Especially now.

THREE

JASON

I walked upstairs to the library. I knew at this time my mother would be reading. I stood in the doorway and stared at her. My mother was a beautiful woman. She had long, black her that was in her usual long braid. She was short with honey skin. She had brown eyes and a face of Dorothy Dandridge.

"If you not going to come in, go and stay away for another couple of years. See if I care." She said to me while reading her book. I smiled at her theatrics. I walked in and stood before her. Her eyes lifted up to mine and there were unshed tears in them. I kneeled before her, took the book out her hand, and placed it on the nearby table. I grasped her hands and kissed them both.

"Hi Momma." I told her. The darkness dissipating.

She placed her hands on my face and gave me that smile that no one else could get from her. "Hey, my baby. Are you back?" She asked with the tears running down her face. I wiped her tears and answered her question that she was really asking. Was I out for good?

"I'm here, Momma. I'm not going anywhere." I told her, calmly and truthfully.

She pulled me into a hug. "Thank you. I have been praying for you to come to your senses. I missed my boy. What have you been up to?" She asked before pulling away. I thought about all the killing, torturing, and all other shit I had been through. I looked her in her eyes and told her the truth. "Work."

"Work, huh." I nodded my head at her question. She looked into my eyes and saw that it was really me. Jason. Not the killer Jason but the son Jason. "Well, since you are back, we will be going to the grocery store on tomorrow. We will have a big dinner. I remember you telling me about the food down south that you love. Maybe you and I can remake those dishes."

"Whatever you want, Ma." I told her. I would give my Mom the world if she asked for it. "How have you been Ma?" I asked her still kneeling.

"I'm better now that my baby is home. Where did you go?" She asked while gripping my beard. I had never let my hair grow like this. My shit was always clean no matter where I was. I'd be in the barbershop tomorrow. I gotta look good parading the Queen around.

"All over Ma, but it doesn't matter now. How about we go to the mall and do some shopping? I know there is some new shit out that you can't wait to get." My mother laughed at my comment. Me and my mom stayed in the mall shopping just because. Buying shit that we didn't need. "Yes indeed, you know your Momma, boy." I stood and pulled up a chair next to her.

"How about we talk? Let's talk like we used to. Talk to me son." She told me staring into my soul. I sighed and rubbed my hands down my face. I was always able to talk to my mom. She passed no judgment. I looked at her and told her all the gruesome shit that I did overseas.

She listened and took in everything I said. When I was done, a heavy weight was lifted off my shoulders. I killed mothers, fathers, sisters, brothers, children, basically anybody that was on the list, had to go. I dreamed of every kill I made. I saw face after face every night.

My mother took my face in her palms and kissed my cheek. "Let that Jason rest a bit. Stay so that I can cook you breakfast. You and your father can watch cartoons, how about that?" She asked me.

"I would love that." I said and stood up. "I'm tired, Momma. I'll see you in the morning. I love you." I told her. She was the only woman that heard them words come out my mouth. I kissed her on the top of her head and walked out the library. I walked down the hall where my old room was. My parents kept my room the same. No one really went in there because they were afraid of what they might find.

I opened the door and pulled off my shirt. I went home to take a shower after fucking oh girl. That's where I was when I received the message from my brother. I dropped in the bed, and for the first time, I fell asleep with no problems.

I woke up the next morning fresh as fuck. I still had a couple of nightmares and the darkness was still lingering, but not so much. I took another shower and went downstairs to join my parents. Jordan and JJ went to their own shit. Ever since them clowns turned eighteen, they were out this bitch. They didn't sleep over and Ma didn't ask. She didn't want any of them hoes that they be fucking with, in her house. Her words.

When I reached the family room, Pops had the television on the cartoon channel. We watched the old school Looney Tunes, with Bugs and Daffy Duck. This was our thing. Watching old or new movies. I took a seat and we laughed like we had never seen this shit before.

Mom came in and brought us our plate of food. Strawberry waffles, with some eggs, bacon, sausage, hash, and a big ass glass of orange juice. We ate and continued watching our shows. It felt just like old times. Mom came in, after me and Pops finished eating, with her purse. We both laughed because her ass couldn't wait to get to the mall. She was going to have to wait a little longer because I had to hit the barbershop asap.

Four hours later, we were in the grocery store shopping for ingredients for some New Orleans Crawfish Etouffee and Rice. I didn't want that box made shit. My mother was on the phone with my aunt who was from down south. We were looking for some Tony's seasoning. This was one of the ingredients that they used to season their chicken with. I was standing by the salt and shit with my mom. We were looking up and down the aisle and still couldn't find it.

"Excuse me, sweetheart, do you know if they have Tony's seasoning here." My mom asked the woman who was passing us by. She turned around, and I swear my dick got hard. Baby girl was beautiful. She looked to be 5'6 with the body of a fit woman. It looked like she had abs and shit. She had naturally curly hair. Her complexion was a smooth caramel. Fuck, man. I have never felt like this at the first sight of a chick before and a nigga was feeling her. She smiled at my mom, and that shit took my breath away. I recovered quickly though. I couldn't let this chick see me sweat.

"No, ma'am. They don't have that up here. That seasoning is only down south. What is it you are trying to make?" She asked in a soft voice. Bruh, this girl looked like a baby doll. Her eyes was sparkling and shit.

"My son was stationed down there and loved the food. He bragged on it so much that I had to see what the fuss was all about. My sister stays in ATL and she is giving me the ingredients to some Crawfish Etouffee and rice. Some well-seasoned fried chicken and sweet cornbread." My mother told the beauty.

"Well, that sounds like a Louisiana meal. I should know because that's where I'm from. I have the ingredients to that at my house. I never leave my state without it. But in my opinion, if you season your flour, your chicken will come out good." She said.

"Oh my, I have never done that before." My mother said all surprised and shit. She stood there thinking real hard. I knew the shit that was about to come out her mouth was going to have me dragging her ass out of here. We didn't know this woman at all and she was about to invite her over to cook for us. My mother always did shit like this. That's how Jordan met Lilly.

"I have a great idea. Since you are from the state where my son adores the food, maybe you can come to the house and help me make a couple of dishes. I would love to learn more about that culture if you don't mind." My mom asked her with excitement.

I told y'all. The woman is crazy. This chick was fine as fuck, but I would murk her ass with no problems. I was shaking my head no when the woman answered. "Yes, I would love to show you some dishes from my hometown. I practically cook almost every day for no one. It would be great to get feedback." She held her hand out towards my mom and introduced herself. "My name is Joel."

My mother took her hand. "My name is Joyce Davis, and this is my son Jason." She said pointing towards me. I didn't grab her hand. I ignored her and turned to my mother.

"She is not coming to the house. You can scratch that shit out." I told my mom. We were into some heavy shit. We didn't need witnesses around to dispose of. Like I said, oh girl was fine, but she wasn't worth losing my family over.

"Jason, don't tell me who I can invite to my house. You ain't that far-gone nigga. You better come to your senses quick before I knock some in you." My mother told me with her hand on her hip. I usually didn't talk to her that way. She knew the business though, but I can understand where she was coming from. My mother didn't have any friends or people that she can be free to talk to. So, her wanting company besides us was understandable but not random mutha-fuckers in the grocery store.

"Ma, you don't even know this woman and you trying to get her to cook for me. Nah Ma, that shit ain't going to fly."

"Well, I don't know y'all either, but I see that your mother is trying to do you a favor. You sound ungrateful." Joel said with too much attitude for me.

I turned back to her with a scowl on my face. "Was I talking to you?"

She put her hands on them hips and lit into my ass. "No nigga, but you were talking about me. So, I have every right to speak. Damn, calm yourself down. I know yo mama raised you better than that." She said staring at me.

"Sho did." My mother said cosigning on that shit. Joel looked back at my mom.

"Ms. Joyce, I would love to come and help you cook some dishes for your disrespectful ass son. I will give you my number and you call me when you are ready, and I'll be there." She told my mom, straight ignoring me now.

"Oh, thank you baby. I really appreciate it. You know, he's not like this normally." My mother said while they exchanged numbers. "We will be going home after this. Expect a call from me within the next hour. I'll text you my address."

"Ok, Ms. Joyce, see you later." She gave my mom a genuinely sweet smile. The shit was almost contagious. Almost. She looked at me and the smile dropped. "Bye." She said and walked past me and bumped my shoulder. The girl was bolder than any nigga I'd encountered.

My mom laughed at my expression. "Yeah, she doesn't give two fucks about who you are." She said and laughed up the aisle.

"She doesn't know me, that's why." I tried to bounce back from getting played.

"I don't think it would matter." She said smiling at me.

FOUR

JORDAN

"Aww shit, baby. Suck that shit." I told Lilly.

My baby woke me up with some bomb ass head. Ain't nothing like waking up to a wet mouth or a wet pussy. My baby was sucking the skin off my shit. I pushed her head down while lifting my hips up going deeper. I felt my shit hit her throat and damn near spilled my shit all in her mouth.

She was moaning and playing with her pussy. "Naw, turn that ass around. Let me taste that pussy baby." She turned without letting my dick go. She put that pussy in my face, and I latched onto that shit quick. She gasped and my dick went deeper into her mouth. "Mm, sit up and ride my face baby." I told her slapping on that juicy ass. She sat up and rode my face like a cowgirl.

"Yaaass, baby. Just like that daddy. Oww, make me come." Lilly said grinding on my face. I love this shit. Pussy was a great start to any nigga day. Especially, if that shit was good. I stuck two fingers in that shit and her pussy clamped on them.

"I'm cumming baby. Don't stop. Don't stop." She started chanting. She was never able to last long like this. Her juices started flowing down my fingers and chin. I slurped that shit up like a

Slurpee. I pushed her ass off me and had her on her knees. I grabbed my dick and gently put that shit in. I knew I was a blessed mutha-fucker and bae needed to get used to my dick. I wasn't no savage ass nigga. Lilly was my heart. So, I didn't mind going slow.

When I was all the way in, I sat in that shit until she started bouncing back. I eased out and in, going at her pace. That shit was so wet, it was making noises. The slower my strokes were the faster she began to move. When she was nice and ready, I grabbed her hips and fucked her good. She grabbed the post at the foot of the bed and met my strokes. I put my hand between her legs and massaged her clit.

"Ahh Jordan. I'm right there, baby." She yelled out for the neighbors to hear.

"Bring that ass back then baby." After three more strokes, we were both letting loose. I fell on the side of her, after pulling out.

"Good morning," she said to me all out of breath. I grabbed her hair and pulled her lips towards mine.

"Great morning." I told her after a hard kiss I planted on her lips. "You must have missed me."

"I did. You were gone all day yesterday and we barely talked. I thought that we could have the day to ourselves. What you think?" She asked. Lilly was beautiful in and out. She was a good girl that had her shit together before I came along. She was a kindergarten school teacher. She was a chocolate chick with short hair. She had a slender face with a small nose. Her eyes were light brown and she had a full set of lips. My girl had long ass legs connected to a round, plump ass. I was in chocolate heaven.

"My mom is giving a dinner for Jason. We will go over there for a while and, after that, whatever you want to do, baby." I told her, rubbing my hand up her legs. She nodded ok and gave me a kiss. I was ready for round two, but my phone started ringing. I reached out and grabbed my phone off the nightstand. It was a message from the Elites. I got up, put my shorts on, and went to the balcony of our home.

"Yes," I answered.

"Gage is out. Shadow is available." The operator told me. I really wanted to make a statement. Shadow's work was good, don't get me wrong. But, Gage's shit was better. The shit needed to be done, though.

"Ok, it's a go." I said and hung up. I walked back in and heard Lilly in the shower. I went into the office, of my home, to check for any new emails. Our family had other businesses to attend to. There was the car dealership, construction, three-night clubs, and a shipping company. We had money in all kinds of stocks. Money was coming in from all angles. Lilly walked in with her towel on with my phone in her hand. "Here, it's JJ." She passed it to me and I slapped her on her ass. She smiled and walked out switching that ass.

"What's up, JJ?" I asked him while I scrolled down my emails.

"Hey, what time are you going to the house?" He asked out of breath.

"Nigga, what are you doing?" I asked him, hoping this nigga didn't call me after fucking one of those broads.

"I just came from my morning run. Tiffany just left the crib. I was going to invite her over, but you know how Jason get when you bring new people by the house. I don't feel like dealing with his shit." JJ said making sense.

When mom brought Lilly over to help her decorate the house, Jason was livid. He stayed attached to them like he was the bodyguard. He did background checks, credit checks, ancestory.com checks, and any other checks he could have come up with. She passed that shit with flying colors and he accepted her as a little sister. He gave me the big brother talk when I told him that I was going to take her out. That nigga grilled me and told me to have her home at a decent hour. Sad part about that was, the nigga was serious.

"Yeah, you know that nigga ain't having that. I'll be over there around seven. I'll probably take Lilly to the house out in the east." I told him, as I walked towards the master bathroom. "Did Pops ask you to bring something?"

"No, just myself and my appetite. You know a nigga ready to eat.

Tiffany can't cook worth of damn. She cooked some shit last night that had my house funky as fuck. I put all the windows up and still can't get that smell out. I banned her ass from cooking until she takes some classes." He said sounding angry.

I started laughing at that fool. He was always getting these broads that couldn't do shit but spend money. Don't get me wrong, the chicks were bad. They just were dumb or just fucking stupid. "Hey, the Elites called and said that Gage was unavailable. We had to go with Shadow." I told him and wanted to change the subject from his block head ass hoes.

"Man, that's fine too. Anyone of them muthafuckers would do. Like Pops said, as long as it wasn't Jason. That nigga looked bad, Jo. We need to bring that nigga to the strip club or something." JJ said to me. Jason had the full-face beard going on. He was dressed down as always, but he just looked raggedy.

"Yeah, we need to do something with our brother. But, it's gon have to be next weekend. I gotta do something with my girl." I told him, as I was getting up and walking towards the bathroom.

"Man, you know if you tell Lilly that Jason need you, she won't trip. Come on man." JJ pleaded with me. I sighed. I prepared the shower and told him that I was going to call him back. I hung up the phone and went to find Lilly. My brother needed me, and I had to be there for him. Lilly was putting lotion on her body. I walked up behind her and wrapped my arms around her. "I need a favor, Baby." I said kissing her on the neck.

"Whatever JJ want you to do it's a no. Fucking around with him you going to get yourself caught up with them dumb ass broads." She said shaking her head.

"It's not JJ. It's Jason. He need-" I was cut off by her lips pressed up against mine.

"Whatever my big brother need? Help him out. It's not often that he needs you. Go, I'll be home waiting on you." My woman told me. That's that shit I liked to hear. No fuss or complaining. "Thank you, Babe."

FIVE

JASON

"Ma, that girl ain't coming over here. Call her back and tell her don't worry about it." I told my mom. She was excited like the top chefs was coming in this bitch. She texted Joel the address to the house. She started pulling out pots, pans, and old ass aprons from way back when. My mother was a beast in the kitchen, but when it was time to learn something new, she perfected that shit with ease.

"Get out of my kitchen with all that noise Jason. She is coming and that is that. Don't be up in here grilling that girl either. Go sit your ass down somewhere." She told me still pulling shit out of the cupboards. I sat down and watched her for about twenty minutes before the phone rang. I picked up the receiver and answered.

"Yeah," I told the security guards that were at the gate of the house.

"There is a Joel Smith here to see Mrs. Davis." Jerome told me. He'd been working for my family for years. He could read people and see shit that was invisible to the normal people. Normal people was like Lilly. She saw the good in everything. I didn't think she belonged with Jordan, but he eased his ass right up in there.

"What you think?" I asked him.

"She good." He said knowing that I was going to do my own investigation.

"Let her through." I said and hung up. I went to the front door to meet Ms. Attitude. When I got to the door, she was getting out her car with bags of shit. She was right though. My mom did raise us to be gentlemen. I walked down the stairs and reached for the bags. She stared at me before giving them to me. "That's all you got." I asked her.

"Yes, that's all I have." She said motioning for me to walk ahead of her. We walked into the house and straight into the kitchen. My mom walked up to her and gave her a hug like they were best buddies. I will have to get her ass a dog or something. She was just too got damn friendly.

"Hey Sweetie, you ready to throw down in this kitchen." My mom asked, walking Joel in the rest of the way.

"Yes, ma'am. I also brought the ingredients for some pecan praline candy. I know you guys will like that." Joel said and smiled at my mom. She wasn't lying. Them praline candies was off the chain. My mouth got watery thinking about that shit. I put the bags down and sat on the stool next to the marble island in the kitchen.

"Are you helping?" Joel asked while grabbing the groceries out the bag.

"No," I told her.

"Then why you in here. Is there a football game on somewhere that you can be watching?" She asked getting all irritated.

"I'm not going nowhere. Cook the shit and get out." I said not giving a fuck about her feelings. She was really getting on my nerves. My mother was about to say something, but Joel beat her to it.

"Look luv, I don't know what your problem is, but you are directing that shit at the wrong person. You are sitting up in here like a guard dog like somebody trying to hurt your momma. I am not that type of person. If you need a brief background, I can give it to you easily. My name is Joel Smith. I have two brothers with no sisters. I am from New Orleans. I am a college graduate and I own my own company called Build It. I have no kids, no spouse, and a deceased mother. I am twenty-three and live alone. There. Happy now. Used that information to get whatever you need and get the fuck." She said in one breathe.

She took the knife off the counter and started chopping up onions. My mother was giggling and chopping up the green bell peppers. I mean, oh girl went off on me. I didn't say anything after that. But, I did store the information she gave me in my head to check her out thoroughly. I sat and watched the women move and talk in the kitchen. The shit looked so natural that you would have thought that they knew each other for years. Jordan and Lilly walked in after a while.

"Damn, Ma, it smells good in here. What you up in here making?" Jordan paused when he saw Joel.

"Thank you, baby, but Joel is up in here working her magic." My mom said smiling. I stood as Lilly was approaching me. I picked her up in a tight hug.

"What you been up to?" I asked her.

"Trying to keep your brother in line. Other than that, I have been dealing with a lot of six-year-old girls and boys." She told me looking me over. Just like my brothers, I know she was worried. I took her hands in mine and looked into her eyes.

"I'm good Lilly." I told her.

"You better be, or I was going to kick your ass." She said with tears in her eyes. We were interrupted with Joel introducing herself to Jordan. "Hi, I am Joel. You must be Jordan." She said and shook his hand, then turned towards Lilly. "You must be Lilly. It is nice to meet you both."

"Oh, hi Joel. You up in here cooking like this." Lilly fell in a conversation with Joel and Mom. Jordan walked up to me with this confused look.

"Where the fuck she come from?" Jordan whispered to me.

"Mom met her in the grocery store and asked her to come over. They been cooking for almost two hours." I told him.

"Ma just be letting anybody in this bitch." Jordan said. He understood where I was coming from. Before anything else was said, Joseph walked in rubbing his stomach.

"Please tell me that the food is almost ready. Ma, you got it smelling like soul food heaven in here." He stopped quickly when he saw Joel. "We got a cook." He asked licking his lips. For some reason, that shit pissed me off. I brushed that shit off and watched his clown ass approach Joel. "My name is Joseph. What are you doing after this?" He asked with a deeper voice than usual.

"My name is Joel, and I am going nowhere, with nobody." She said shutting that shit down. I smiled a little. This nigga was always trying to fuck something. My Pops finally walked in after a nap and greeted everyone. When he got to Joel, he did his usual look over. He was another one who can read people. He grabbed her hand and shook it gently. He didn't see anything as well. "Will you be staying for dinner." He asked her still holding her hand.

"Sure, if it's okay with the Guard." She said and looked at me. Pops dropped her hand and turned towards me.

"You and that fucking mouth." I said. I stood up and walked out the kitchen. Before I could get out the door, she responded.

"I know. It's lethal, ain't it?"

My brothers and father stared at me and waited for a response. No one talked back to me like that. What my brothers and father had witnessed, was pure nonsense. This girl had to have a death wish fucking with me. I turned to stare at her and she stared back. I mean, she didn't blink at all. "Don't sit yo ass next to me." I said walking out.

I went to my room to check my phone for messages. I had missed calls from Mya asking me to come over again. I didn't want to give oh girl hope. I might have to cut her off. She was getting too attached and shit. I put my phone down and headed back downstairs where everybody was sitting at the table.

The dining room was big as fuck. My mother always wanted to have family gatherings with grandkids and shit. Jo and Lilly were the only hope my mother had. JJ and I were not ready for no kids, like I said before. Shit, I wasn't ready for a relationship. Three other people joined us for dinner. It was Jeff, Rick, and Brian. They were some guys that we grew up with. They were all older than I was but treated me no different.

"What's up Jason?" Jeff spoked. We were the closest. He taught me some shit that I used while I was away. I gave him a half hug and shook his hand. "Nothing man, chilling. How you been?"

"Cooling, bout to grub it up with y'all and that fine ass broad." He said staring at Joel.

"Not that one my nigga." I told him seriously. He was a dog just like Joseph. She didn't need to be with any of us.

"Aight, you got that." He said walking towards the table. It was full of food. Shit, I didn't even ask for was sitting on this table. I greeted the rest of the crew and sat next to my mother. Joel was sitting in between Rick and JJ. Two savage ass niggas. Rick was with his girl Brittany and they had a beautiful little girl name Saniya. He was never faithful, and that shit bothered me. Why get into a relationship with someone, just to not see her with another dude? Joel kept it real and held her own, though. Anything that them fools was throwing, she threw that shit back at them with sass.

"The food was delicious Joel." My father complimented her and fixed another plate.

"Thank you, Mr. Jordan. I enjoyed cooking with Ms. Joyce." She looked towards my mom. "Anytime you need me in that kitchen with you, just call."

"You just made a best friend, Joel. Joyce will be calling you on tomorrow." My pops told her. We all agreed that the food was great. I don't know about this coming over everyday shit, though. We all started removing dishes from the table and brought them to the kitchen. The women started cleaning up while the men went to the back patio.

"We are going to the strip club tonight nigga, and you coming with us. We gotta get you some pussy quick. You sitting all straight and shit, like we in one of those 'how to be a lady' classes." Joseph said out of the blue. I looked at that fool like he was crazy. That's all this nigga thought about.

He was with a different bitch, every three days. He said that was his limit. I heard he was messing with some new chick that he was thinking about bringing over before I came home to meet Mom, but he never did. I was not going to no bum ass strip club though. Pussy was not a high priority for me. I can get the shit whenever I wanted. So, I wasn't desperate for it. "Pussy ain't the answer to everything nigga."

They all stared at me in disbelief. Pops came and put his hand on my head to check if I had a fever. "Shiidd." They all said laughing at me. I couldn't do nothing but laugh with them fools. I missed this shit. I missed my brothers. We were talking about crew shit, when Lilly walked out with Joel.

"Hey babe, Joel is going to teach me how to make your favorite on tomorrow. So, I'll be over here after I get off from work." Lilly told Jordan smiling.

"Are you a cook or something?" Brian asked.

"No, I love to cook. In the south, we were taught to cook at an early age. My mother had me in the kitchen every night. We cooked holiday dinners, birthday dinner, or just Sunday dinners. I was the only girl. My mother raised me to take care of myself and the family I was going to have." She answered Brian.

"Look, fuck all that, are you single? Me and you can make that family yo momma was preparing you for." Rick said walking towards Joel. I stood up to block that nigga's advances. He looked me up and down like I was small. "Come on, J, I know you not blocking." He said to me, while trying to get around me. I leaned my head to the side to see if this nigga really wanted it with me.

"Yes, I am single, but I don't want no trifling ass boy." She said to Rick, which had them laughing. Rick was a sneaky muthafucker. I didn't trust him like the other two. He was jealous of what we had. You can see it all over that nigga's face when he came around. I definitely didn't want him around Joel. He was barely allowed in the house. I looked towards JJ for him to act quick before I do. He got up to grab his boy because he was about to get fucked up. I turned towards Joel to ask her a question.

"Where you stay?"

"Why you want to know?" She asked with her face all scrunched up.

"Because I want to know. Can you answer one simple question without giving me that attitude?"

"Nope, because it's none of your business where I stay. I don't want your stalking ass around my house." She said walking around me like I was an invalid. "Goodnight everyone. Lilly, I'll see you tomorrow." She turned and past me again bumping my shoulder. "Bye." She said over her shoulder.

"It looks like you met your match, big brother." Lilly said in a taunting tone.

"Shut up," I told her as she laughed. My brothers and the guys were staring at me. I ignored them and walked inside. I told my parents good-bye and went to my SUV. It looks like I'll be paying Mya a visit tonight fucking around with Joel.

SIX

JORDAN

A few weeks went by and a lot has been going on. DJ was returned home to his parents, but the other guys were dead. I went to see how he was doing and they fucked him up. He was missing an ear and six of his fingers. He gave me the rundown on how everything went, and the shit was disturbing. I received the receipt for my orders from the Elites and Shadow really did his thing. No one survived that hit. He took out all the males that were in the family. He left the house painted with blood. After I received that and let DJ know that we handled it, I went over to our nightclub uptown.

It was called D1. It was the biggest and the most popular one out of the three. The club was a warehouse with three levels. The first floor was for the younger crowd that liked to get crunked and shit. The second floor was for the laid-back crowd. The third floor was strictly for business and family. I walked in and went straight through the side door that was only used by me and JJ. Jason didn't come here much. The nigga didn't do well with crowds. I went to the third floor and started working on liquor orders. I counted the cash for the deposit and went over some other shit.

After all that shit was done, I left the club after staying there for four hours. I saw that I would have to hire some management. We had some women managers before, but Joseph fucked them all. I was walking to my car when there were two figures approaching me. These niggas must not have known. I pulled out my nine and started shooting without waiting for them to act first. I hit both of them fools with ease. I walked over to see who the fuck was trying to run up on me.

I hit one of them in the head. "No answers from you. Let's see what yo pussy ass gotta say." I kicked the other in the face. I shot him in the shoulder and this bitch was crying like he was dying. "The fuck is you, nigga?" I asked him with my gun pointed to his face.

"Don't worry about who I am, bitch. Know that you and your family is about to get dealt with. Y'all always in other people business. Fuck you, nigga." That clown said and spat at me.

Time out for a second.

That had to be the most disrespectful shit ever. Don't be spitting at me, bruh. That shit had me seeing red. I stomped that nigga head in the ground. Joseph ran up to me and pulled me back from the dude.

"Jo! Jordan calm down!" He said breaking me out my daze. "What the fuck is going on?" He asked me while staring down at the two idiots that ran up on me.

"Some punk ass niggas talking shit." I said taking off my shoes. These were a brand-new pair of Timbs that bitch fucked up.

"Where they come from, Jo? Did you get any answers from him?" JJ continued with his interrogation.

"He said something about us not minding our business and that we were going to be dealt with. Call the crew and meet me at the center. I will call Pops and Jason." I told him getting in my car after tossing my shoe in the truck. "Call for a cleanup," was the last thing I said before I peeled off in my 2017 Ford Mustang V6. I heard a couple of more shots after that. I knew that JJ couldn't resist letting off a couple of shots on them already dead fools. I called my father first. He answered all sleepy and shit. "Yes, Son."

"Pops, I believe that there is a hit put on the family. I'm on my way to the center. Is Jason with you?" I asked him. I heard a lot of shuffling on his side. It sounds like he was getting up from sleeping.

"No, he is not. I will call him. Go and set up for the meeting. I'll be there in a minute." He said hanging up.

He was really trying to keep Jason out of this mess. He has been chilling with my mom and Joel. The shit was funny to watch. Jason would say something to her and she would say something back more vicious. That shit had him speechless. Lilly had been going over there ever since that night after dinner. She brought home something new every night. I wasn't complaining. I was gaining a lot of weight from that shit though. I pulled up to another warehouse we owned. When I pulled up, the whole crew was there except my father and Jason. I went into the office and retrieved another pair of Timbs. When I came back down, Jason and my father were walking into the door.

"I was attacked tonight by some punk ass bitches telling me that my family was going to get dealt with. The only thing that can put us in this shit was helping Derrick's crew. We gotta keep our eyes open for any unexpected guests. If you see something suspicious, handle that shit and we will find the answers out later. They won't talk anyway. I want more guards at my parents' house. Jason will be there so y'all follow his protocol. Craig, I want you guarding Lilly. Don't be all obvious nigga, be discrete. If any of you fuck up, don't bother coming back. Jason will come to see you. Any questions?" I asked the group of men who have been loyal to me and the fam since day one. The all nodded their heads and got up to handle business.

My brothers and father lingered a little to continue with the discussion. "What the fools look like?" Jason asked. You can see murder already in this fool's eyes. He was about to lose it. Somebody had put a bid out on our family and it was time for all of us to show out.

"Some yellow ass nigga with a mouth full of platinum, aluminum, or whatever the fuck that was in his mouth. Bitch spit on me too. I tried to put that hoe in the concrete." I said getting more upset.

"Are you serious?" Jason asked getting all fired up too. "Please tell me you fucked him up?" This nigga sounds like he was begging.

"What the fuck I look like? I split the nigga skull open." I told him.

"He not lying. I had to keep that nigga from going over. He was foaming at the mouth and shit." JJ said while imitating me. He was growling and bust out laughing.

We all did.

"Well, I'm going to get in touch with my contacts and try to find out all about the Mitchell's. If someone out there trying to get revenge, it can be somebody real close to the family. Did you ask for a blackout when you put in the order?" Jason asked staring at the wall above my head. I hate when he does that shit. You gotta snap your fingers at him to get his attention.

"No, I didn't think it was necessary." I told them. Fuck, I really didn't. Them bitches wasn't about that life. Fucking with Derrick and his fam was a minor infraction. It's a whole different game when you start a war with us.

"Ok, I'm on it." Jason said walking away.

"No, you won't Jason. Stand down son. Just contact your people; we will handle the rest. Ok." Pops told him. Ever since Pops stepped down, I had made all the decisions without his input. I understood what Pops was trying to do, but I needed the killer Jason.

"Pops, I'm good. I can control myself." Jason told pops tiredly.

"No, the fuck you can't." We all said together.

Jason looked at us like we didn't know him. His eyebrows rose up like he needed to be reminded. We all started talking at once, but JJ's story was a prime example of him losing control.

"Do you remember the dude that bumped you in the club downtown? Dude said my bad and everything. You fucked him and his crew up. Then you went to the parking lot, found his car, and shot that bitch up. Nah, nigga, you can't control yourself. Keep on chilling with Ma and Joel." Joseph told him.

"Hell no. Joel is going to make a muthafucker choke her ass up. I told her that I was going to follow her home to make sure she gets there safe. She told me to follow my ass down the yellow brick road and ask the Oz for a sense of humor. She said I be blowing her and shit." This nigga said smirking a bit. I don't give a fuck what nobody says, his ass was feeling Joel. More than he wanted to.

"When you get the information, put a blackout hit on the family. Make sure Gage is available this time. He will send you pics and shit." Pops told me. We used Gage a lot due to his techniques. When the body is discovered after his hit, it is drained of the blood and organs. The medical examiner was able to tell the victim's family- if there were any left- that they suffered. Severely.

"Yeah, I'll make sure this time. Everybody just go home. We will talk about this tomorrow. Dinner by you Pops." I asked him.

"Yep. Joel is making Gumbo." He said rubbing on his stomach. We all looked forward to dinners now. We felt like royalty for real.

"Aight, I'll see y'all later." I walked out the center with my family, jumped in my car, and went home to Lilly. Hopefully, she was up. If not, she was about to be.

SEVEN

JASON

"I'm not playing with you Jason. Go and pick that food up from Joel's house. She said the gumbo was done and she was making the potato salad right now." My mother screamed through the speakers of my SUV. I told her ass that she didn't have to talk that loud.

"Ma, I'm not going over there. Let her bring that shit herself." I said. She was aggravating the fuck out of me. She has been trying to get me to go over there for thirty minutes now. I didn't want to be bothered, especially with trying to get the information on the fools that put a bid out on my family.

"Ok, I'll just ask Joseph and Ricky to go over there." She said in a rush to hang up.

"I'll go! I'll go! Damn, you gonna do me like that." I told her. She must have noticed how upset I got when them fools flirted with her.

"I'll let her know that you are on your way." She told me like her plan went through.

I knew where Joel lived. I looked that shit up her first day over. Matter fact, I was on my way regardless. I pretended like I wasn't interested in Joel. I didn't feel like hearing these fools mouth about how I was acting off pussy I didn't get yet. And then, it was the fact that I was feeling something, besides anger, for someone that wasn't family. She be having me smiling and smirking and shit. Sad thing about that is, she does it so effortlessly.

I pulled up to her home and heard the music blasting. I went to knock on her door and the shit was open. I pulled out my gun and walked in. The foyer was small with an overhead picture of the French Quarters in New Orleans. The music was coming from the left of the house. I cautiously looked around and continued walking through before I saw her in the kitchen. She was bouncing to some rap song. Livid wasn't the right word to describe how I was feeling. I was ready to yoke her ass up fa real.

"Are you fucking crazy? You just leave your door open fa mutha-fuckers to walk in and snatch yo ass up." I yelled at her.

"Look, don't come in my house with yo bad vibes nigga. Ma-Ma told me you were on your way. I unlocked the door for you, so that I wouldn't have to stop doing what I was doing. Grab that pot with the pot holders. Place that towel on the floor of your car and place that Gumbo on there. Come back in and get this potato salad and then carry your angry looking ass out my house." She told me without a care in the world. She was still mumbling shit under her breath about how I was getting on her nerves.

The girl didn't even turn around to say that shit to my face. That shit bothered me. I was about to walk over there, until she turned and gave me that "I wish you muthafuckin would" look. It put me on pause, but I recovered quickly. She had me slipping in many ways. The shit intrigued me on the slick. She didn't give a fuck what, how, or when she gave me that attitude of hers. It didn't matter how I reacted; she took that shit like a G and kept that shit pushing. I'm going to have to fix that mouth though.

I turned around to pick up the pot off the counter, when I saw and smelled a lemon cake. As you all can tell, I got a sweet tooth. Pies, cakes, candy, and any other sweets were my weakness. The cake was round with lemon shavings on it. Straight jacked move.

"Hey, I'm bringing this cake too." I wasn't asking.

"Take a piece and tell me what you think. That is the first time I baked that one." She said again with her back turned. She didn't have to tell me twice. I took the knife that was sitting next to it and cut a big ass slice. I bit into that shit and could have sworn I saw heaven. This had to be the best I ever had. Another bite and it was gone. I cut another smaller piece and ate it slower to really enjoy the flavor. I was chewing and listening to the music that she was playing.

"What are you listening to?" I asked cutting another piece.

"J. Cole and Kendrick Lemar mix."

"Who?" I said chewing on the last piece. She repeated it slower like that was going to make me know who them niggas were. "Man, they not talking about nothing."

She turned around like I told her I didn't believe in Jesus. "Who you listen to?"

"Pac, Nas, Biggie, and other old school rappers." I replied to her while cutting another piece.

"Those are some of the rappers that they admire. They talk about real life nigga shit." She said after turning the music up.

"How you know? You not a dude."

"I do have brothers, fool."

THROWIN BLOWS FIGHTING demons trying to stop from bustin semen

In an unfamiliar bitch I know my niggas feel this shit
How could I fuck her raw? And I just met the ho
My dick took over it ain't never felt this wet before

I STOPPED and listened to what dude was saying and he was saying some real shit. I ain't gon even lie, that shit happened to me once or twice. Nigga was drunk as fuck both times. I was nodding my head understanding every word to every song that came on.

"You must have liked the cake." Joel said staring at me for however long.

I looked at the plate and that bitch was empty. "It was alright." I told her.

She busted out laughing. "That shit was more than alright. You ate that cake like you was a judge of Cake Boss, nigga. What you talking bout?"

I closed my mouth quickly, when I caught myself laughing with her. "Hey, can you send that playlist to my phone." I said getting up. "Do you need to bring anything else to the house?"

"No, that is everything, and yes, I'll send you that playlist." She said wiping down the counters.

"Are you coming over?"

"Why, so that you can lock the door?" She answered me, jokingly and seriously at the same time.

"Naw, I was going to save you a seat." I told her. I was standing in front her, waiting for her answer.

"Yeah, I'll be there for six-thirty. Don't sit me next to frit and frat please." She said still cleaning up the mess she made.

"Cool, I got you." I told her and brought the food to my car. I got to my parents' home and took a shower. The guys were already there, and Lilly was in the kitchen with my mom. We didn't like talking about business around mom. She knew the business as well as everyone else, but dinner time was just that, dinner time. We all were sitting around the table around seven and there still weren't no signs of Joel. I was about to call when she came walking through the door with a dress on. The shit clung on to all her curves. Her titties and ass were sitting up nice in that dress. Fuck! I wanted to lay her out on this table.

"You know what time it is?" I asked her while standing up.

"You clocking my time now." She said with an attitude.

"That mouth. That fucking mouth. Ju-Just come sit your ass down so we can eat." I pulled the chair out next to me.

"Did you put something in my food or drink. Wait, I know, you put tacks in my seat." She said walking cautiously. When she got to the seat, she examined it and her food on the plate I made. Everyone was looking at us waiting for the entertainment that we always give during dinner time. We talked and had an enjoyable conversation this time. We talked about our childhood and how fucked up I was back then.

"Jason didn't get along with none of his teachers. He was an intelligent kid. But, when he would finish his work, he would get bored." Pops told her. "I had to go to the school many of times because he walked out or just was interrupting the class."

Joel was about to say something when her phone went off. She took it out of her bag, looked at it, and frowned. "Shit, I gotta go." She said getting up. "One of my clients is having trouble with his business."

"I'll walk you out." I said standing as well. My brothers' jaws dropped after that comment. Ma and Pops smiled at us. I ignored them and led Joel out after she said her goodbyes to my parents. When we got outside, I took her hand and lead her to the car. "Don't forget to send that playlist to me."

"I guess them niggas was talking about sumthin." She said nudging me with her shoulder.

"Yeah, they were aight."

"Yeah, whatever, but I won't forget. I'll send it as soon as I get home."

"Are you coming over tomorrow?" I asked her.

"What is wrong with you? First, you can't wait to get me out the house. Now, you trying to keep me at the house." She said confusedly.

I didn't know what to tell her. But, what I did know, was that her lips were calling me and I ain't a kissing nigga. I didn't know how these hoes were operating now. They be quick to suck dicks and brag about it. I know that Joel wasn't like that. Baby girl had standards. I got closer to her to get in position to take what I wanted. I never deprive myself of anything. Why should I start now?

I grabbed her face and took her bottom lip into my mouth. Her lips were so soft. That shit surprised me. I sucked on it and tasted the sweetness of it. I let her lip go and pushed my tongue into her mouth. She moaned, and that shit turned me on. I cuffed her ass and lifted her off the ground. My hands were under her dress caressing her shit. Her skin was smooth and soft as silk. She started grinding on my dick through my jeans and sucking on my tongue. I was losing my fucking mind in front of my parents' house. I put her down and leaned my forehead to hers. I didn't want my parents to see us out here like this.

"What time are you coming for?" I asked out of breath.

"Four," she replied out of breath as well.

"Be here at four, do you hear me? The shit won't be pretty if I have to come and get you. You understand?" I told her and meant every word.

"Yes," she said simply. No back talk or attitude. I think I have found the cure for that fucking mouth.

"If me putting my tongue down your throat get you to act right, I guess I gotta do it more often." I told her. I placed a softer kiss on her lips and pulled back. I opened her door and closed it when she got in. "Call me when you get home, no text."

She nodded and pulled off.

I had to wait before going back in. Them niggas will clown me fo sho if I walked in with three legs. After a couple minutes passed, I went back into the house to finish off the night with my family. I was feeling calm and at peace. I haven't felt this way in a while. We continued joking and reminiscing the rest of the night. I forgot some of the things that were brought up and how I was slowly becoming the asshole I grew up to be. My mother retired to her bedroom while we went to the office with my father. We were talking about the status of all this shit that's been happening when the phone rang. Jordan answered it and put it on the TV screen above the fireplace.

"Jordan, how are you?" The speaker asked.

When I looked up to the screen, I saw that it was this lame ass dude I went to school with. Bitch was so lame he moved away to get a new start.

"Why are you on my line, bruh?" Jordan asked nonchalantly.

"I thought you wanted to know who I was. I have been hearing that you was looking for the one that put that bid on your fam. Damn, you niggas are ungrateful like a muthafucker." He said, trying to make sense of his phone call.

This nigga was fa real. I was wasting good contacts and time on this hoe ass fuck boy. I was texting my boy to cancel that order. I can find his ass without all this shit. Not as quick, though.

"I know you lying. Bitch, when I catch you, I'm going to fuck you up myself. You playing with the right ones this time." JJ said getting mad as well. We really thought we were preparing for some heavy hitters. I didn't have time for this shit. I was going to pass on Joel and see how wet that pussy could get for me.

"That's y'all problem right there. Always underestimating the underdogs. You niggas keep on. Your family is marked." He said digging a bigger hole for him and his fam.

Jordan stood and stared up at the screen. I wasn't gon' lie. My big brother was someone you needed to fear. Especially when it came to the family. "Look here, bitch. I don't care if you were the top dog, you still don't invoke fear over here. As you can see, this family is well-guarded. Bring yo weak ass on and get fucked up if you want to. Cuz clearly you don't know who you fuckin with."

"Oh, so you say. But, I was told that you guys have a new member of the family." He told us. We were all thinking about who he could be talking about and nothing came up. "Confused. Well, I guess she doesn't mean anything to y'all. Maybe she can come to my house and cook for me. You know, after the crew fuck her good. I don't think you hitting that right Jason."

My head popped up and this nigga was actually smiling at me. I felt all the calmness I had during these couple of weeks dissolve. I stared at that nigga with nothing but rage. You can tell that he didn't have the same confidence he had at the beginning of this call. "When I catch you, nigga, it's over for you and your family." You can see the sweat rolling down this hoe ass nigga's face. Y'all see what I'm saying. He wasn't made for this shit. Before anything else could happen, something came to mind. I pulled my phone out to check for any missed calls. FUUUCK!

I stormed out the house and ran to my car. I heard my pops tell him that he'd just fucked up and he did. I called Joel's phone and it kept going to voicemail. I smashed my phone on the steering wheel. If anything, happened to her, I promised that life wasn't going to be the same for that nigga. I was thinking of ways to kill his whole family. The stepchildren and all.

I pulled up to Joel's house and it was dark as fuck. I didn't waste time knocking or ringing the doorbell. I kicked the door off the hinges with no weapon. Nah, these niggas were going to suffer fucking with her. I was on my way to her bedroom when she came out in a wife beater and some boy shorts.

"Jason, what the fuck is your problem? You must be smoking that shit busting through my house like this?"

I straight ignored her and moved through that bitch. I was on a mission. If she knew what was best for her, she would get the fuck out of my way. When I was done searching her house, she was still ranting. I took her by the shoulders and shook her.

"Pack your shit, you're coming with me."

"What's wrong, Jason. Is everything alright? Ma-Ma. Pops. Your brothers." She said as her voice changed from aggravation to being concerned.

"Everyone is good. I just need you to do as I say. Don't argue with me aight. Pack your pots, pans, flour, and whateva else you need so that we can go." I said. I saw that she was still worried. I caressed her face and kissed her lips. I was happy that I got there in time. I pulled back and watched her let out a deep breath.

"Ok, Jason. But, you are going to explain everything to me when we get in the car." She said walking off.

"Put some clothes on too. What the fuck you sleeping in?" I told her

"I don't have to explain shit to you. You don't pay not one fuckin bill in this bitch and you ain't my nigga." She told me, once again mumbling shit under her breath.

I shook my head and waited for her to pack her shit. I went into the car to grab my other phone I kept stored for emergencies. I called my contact while scoping out her place again. "I need an ASAP on the order. When can you have it for me?" I asked while I was walking back into her house.

"I'll have the info in a day." He responded.

"Curtis Harris is the name of the bitch behind this. That should make it twelve hours. I'll be waiting." I said and hung up the phone. I was looking out the window when Joel came down the stairs in some joggers and a half shirt sweater shit with her stomach out. I let out a sigh. This fucking woman.

"Damn, Hulk, you couldn't try to fix my got damn door. I kinda like my shit, ya know." She said while carrying her bag and ignoring my attitude to her outfit.

"Look, I'll get somebody to fix that door. But, you don't got a whole shirt or sweater to put on." I grilled her.

"Didn't you tell me to hurry up? You weren't specific about my outfit nigga. We either goin or you can board up my door and we stay here. I ain't changing J." She said putting her hand on her hip. She was unbothered by the look I was giving her too. I grabbed her bag and walked out to the car. I drove back to the house thinking of the ways that I was going to make Curtis suffer with more than his life.

EIGHT

JORDAN

Curtis was a whole hoe outchea. He's playing with the right ones like I said. Lilly went upstairs to our old room. We weren't leaving the house tonight. After Jason left, we got prepared to take out his whole family. Joel was family now and my father was going crazy. He saw her as his daughter. Shit, she spent enough time here. If Mom was to find out that Joel has been threatened, she would pull out her own gun. Joseph called the rest of our crew over to discuss the plans. I already knew where Curtis' people were staying. I started talking about the plans when Jason walked in with Joel.

My father got up and hugged her tightly. "I am so glad that you're okay, sweetheart. You are to stay here until we figure this shit out. No ifs, ands, or buts about that." He said to her in that fatherly tone. The one that we usually get when Pops meant for you to do as you were told. Joel nodded her head at Pops and the rest of the guys. She turned to leave, but Jason stopped her.

"Go to my room upstairs, the third door to your left. I will be up in a minute." He told her.

"Ok, where are you sleeping?" She asked him with that attitude that was going to get the piss slapped out of her.

Jason frowned up at her question. "In the same room, what the fuck you think?"

"I am not sleeping in the same room with you. Get the fuck out of here. I'll sleep in the guest room near Ma-Ma and Pops' room." She said thinking that is was final.

Jason stepped in front of her and we leaned back but forward trying not to seem all obvious and shit about their conversation. The veins in that nigga's neck started popping out. We knew he was trying to calm down from all the shit that was going on. Joel didn't know the buttons that she was pressing was going to cause her-her ass.

Jason grabbed her by the neck and pulled her closer to him. JJ was about to intervene, but Pops stopped him. Jason kissed her softly then whispered to her. "Go to the fucking room and don't make me ask you again." Joel stepped back and walked up the stairs without another word.

"So, that's why we couldn't sit next to her at dinner. Nigga, you were feeling her this whole time." JJ asked him while laughing.

Jason nodded his head. "That's me right there."

JJ walked up to him and dapped him up. "That's what up, nigga. Proud of you bruh."

"Nigga, you can't handle a woman like Joel. Slide that pussy this way J. Let me train her fa you." Rick said to Jason too comfortably. Jason didn't fuck with Rick like that. This nigga was about to get bodied making comments like that about Joel.

I was about to punch his ass in the face, but Jason grabbed that bitch by his throat and slammed him into the wall. We all were standing to see what Jason was going to do to him. We weren't going to stop him. We were lining up to fuck him up too. Even Pops wanted in on some of that action.

"One more fucking time, nigga, and it's over for you. You will see the side of me that the muthafuckers told you about." Jason angrily told him. I don't know what Jason was squeezing, but it had Rick gurgling.

"Fa real, Rick, what's your problem? You been acting funny

nigga." JJ asked him. He was angrier at Rick than we were. This was his boy that he brought into the fam.

"Nah, let that nigga keep trying me. He got his one and final warning. He should feel lucky that he got that. Some don't." Jason said deadly calm. He threw that nigga to the floor and stepped over him like he was trash on the ground.

Zeek walked in with three other guys. He was one of the younger dudes that was accepted into the fam. His older brother Mike was killed last year by some uptown niggas. I promised his mother that I would watch over him after that. We sent Gage to take out the whole uptown crew. That was my first hit I put out before I became the leader of the Davis crew. Zeek fell right in place, just like Mike did.

"Ashton and his family were wiped out. We went to pick him up for the meeting and the cops were surrounding the area. I talked to the neighbor to get the info. She said that they have been dead for two days. His little sister Qiana found them in the family room." He said shaking his head.

"Everyone be at the center before sunrise. It's time for war." I said to the group. I was tired of all this talking and ready for some action. Everyone started walking out to get rest, pussy, or whatever them niggas do before a hit. I went upstairs to be with Lilly. When I walked in the door, she was sitting on the bed reading on her kindle.

I sat on the bed and took it out of her hand to get her attention. She was always reading those books from SP productions. She used to read some of those stories to me that had me wondering what them authors were going through. The shit be fiya though.

"What time are you leaving?" Lilly asked me. She knew the shit I was in. I was different from my father. I talked to Lilly about everything that goes on with the family business. I didn't want her to be blindsided by none of my bullshit.

"We will be leaving at five. Jason and Pops will be here with you guys on the inside. We will have men surrounding the house. I need you to call in tomorrow, that way I know that you are safe."

"Shit, Jordan, I told you that I can handle what you do. But, I don't want your shit to interfere with my job. This will be my third time calling out this month. They need to know that I am a reliable worker." She fussed.

This was always an issue with us. I told her that she didn't have to work, but she started complaining about having her own money and shit. Don't get me wrong, I applauded her work ethics. It was hard guarding a fucking elementary school.

"Do what I say, Lilly. Don't make shit harder than it already is. I don't need us arguing right before we do this hit. Can you please save that shit for another time? Damn!" I told her getting mad. I stood up to go to the adjoined shower that was in my room. This shit she was spitting was for the birds.

I turned the shower on, got undressed, and jumped in. The shower door opened, and Lilly jumped in with me. "I'm sorry, Jordan. I get so nervous when you go on hits like this one. I'm scared baby." She said wrapping her arms around me. I turned in her arms and kissed her with the love I knew she needed to feel.

I know that I wasn't your regular nine to five dude. Even them fools can get shot at any time. Bullets don't choose who they want to hit. I couldn't make her promises that I knew damn well I couldn't keep. I started kissing on her neck and grabbing on her apple ass. She started moaning and stroking my dick. She stepped back and got on her knees. She placed my man in her mouth and went to work.

"Shit," I groaned out. I grabbed her hair to keep her head steady while I slid in and out her mouth. She was driving me crazy. She dropped her hands into her lap and relaxed her throat. She knew that this was what I needed, and she didn't disappoint.

We finished up in the shower and continued in the bed. I woke up later that morning to a knocked-out Lilly. Baby girl was so tired after our session. I got dressed and kissed Lilly on her forehead. I knew that shit could go left, but I was prepared for that. I went downstairs to meet Jason and Joseph in the kitchen with my parents. Joel and Mom was up with breakfast already on the table.

"Good morning, fam. You ready," I asked JJ.

"Yeah, let's get this shit over with quick. I got other shit to do."
Joseph replied.

I grabbed some bacon and walked out with JJ behind me. We
jumped in the Impala that Jason got for this hit and pulled off. "Hey,
what's with yo boy Ricky. That nigga been on one lately." I asked JJ.

Ricky and JJ been hanging with each other since they were kids.
When JJ brought him around the first time, Jason wasn't feeling him
at all. He said that he was a snake in disguise. We didn't agree
because the nigga never showed us different and Jason didn't trust
anyone but family. Rick killed and robbed with us too. Whatever we
had, he had. This new shit Rick was doing had me on one fa real.

"Man, I don't know. That nigga has been tripping." JJ said getting
mad all over again. "I wanted to hit his ass in the throat for saying shit
like that about Joel. He lucky that Jason didn't fuck him up. Nobody
would have complained about it either."

"Yeah, just watch his ass. Don't let him know about anything new
that is going on with the fam. Keep his ass in the dark until we can
figure that shit out." I told him as we were pulling up at the center.
All the cars were parked in the back as usual. We got out and met
everyone inside. Everyone was there but Ricky and Zeek. I wasn't
worried because we had to focus on the job.

"Don, you and your crew take the family uptown. Don't leave no
one alive. Dog, cats, and any other pets them bitches have. Dead
them too. You understand. We will get the downtown family. I want
the hoe ass nigga that started this shit. If Curtis' dad would have
made his mom swallow, his punk ass wouldn't be here starting shit." I
told the crew.

We loaded up and everyone got into their cars. Joseph rode with
the other crew while the rest of the gang rode with me. I was ready to
strangle these dudes. That's why I told my crew to invoke fear in
these niggas. If they did, this shit wouldn't be happening. I know that
Jason was joking about me putting weak ass people on the payroll.
But when I look at how shit was going, all I can do is agree with him.

I pulled up to the two-story house where Curtis' closest relatives were. There was no need to hide our cars because this was our territory. Muthafuckers knew what would happen if they talked to them people around here. I stepped out of the car and waited for Joseph. This nigga was walking up to me rubbing on his stomach.

"Damn man, I should've ate before this shit. I'm hungry as fuck. Do you have chips or something in that bitch?" He asked pushing me aside to go into my center console. That nigga knew I had that shit stashed in there. Why ask? He opened the bag of chips while the guys got out and waited for instructions. We knew how JJ would get if he didn't have anything to eat. I told JJ's crew to hit the side and back of the house. My crew was going in the front door.

JJ finished and led his crew through the side gate. I waited until JJ reached the back to bust the front door down. We heard all the moving around upstairs and in the basement. I signaled JJ's crew to go check downstairs and I went upstairs with my crew. When I reached the top step, Curtis' brother Steve came running out his room. I blasted his ass with that sawed off. He flew back to a door that his father came out of. More gunshots and people screaming was heard throughout the house. "What the fuck is going on?" The older gentleman said.

"Where Curtis at?" I asked the man.

"Fuck you. I ain't telling you shit. Get the fuck out my house." He said with no fear. He was at least 6 feet tall and weighed about 275. I was taller than he was, but he outweighed me by 45 pounds. I wasn't tripping though. His ass was about to get this work.

His wife was on the ground cradling their dead son. I raised my gun and shot her in the head. The man yelled and charged at me. I passed Duke my gun and punched the bitch in his forehead. He stumbled, but came back quick. We were going at it when the rest of the crew came up the stairs. I picked his ass up and slammed him on the table that was against the wall. I grabbed my shit from Duke and shot that bitch in his face. We all walked back downstairs and out the door. The crew shot up six people downstairs. We all got into the car, when my phone rung. "Is it done," I asked Don on the other end.

"Yeah, it's done, but bad news boss. We found Zeek dead in his car in front of Curtis' people house." Don told me.

"Fuck," I yelled hitting my steering wheel.

NINE

JASON

I just got the news about Zeek. I didn't know how I felt about the shit until I found out why he was in front that house. Call it what you want. My family will always be number one. If that nigga was on some fuck boy shit, then he deserved every bullet. I was in the study listening to these niggas talk about retaliation and the shit was pissing me off. Find out if the nigga was loyal to you first before putting your life on the line. They were talking all that rah-rah shit like they really knew him.

"Man, we gotta get them bitches. They not getting away with this shit. My boy didn't deserve this shit." One of the little niggas said. This shit had my head hurting. I got up to walk out the door until the lil nigga stopped me. "Hey, J man, you gotta go and get them niggas. You can't let them get away with this."

I looked at Jordan and JJ. They all were staring at me for a response. I continued walking out of the office. I went to look for my Mom and Joel because sitting in that room was depressing as fuck. They were in the kitchen, as always. My father was sitting at the kitchen island stuffing his face with everything Joel cooked.

I slept peacefully in her arms last night. It's been a long time since I have been able to sleep like that. She started feeding me and I was loving the attention she was giving me.

The men were getting louder and more rowdy. My father looked at me like I knew why. I really didn't want to go back in there. Joel picked up two trays and walked towards the office with me behind her. I grabbed the trays, while Joel opened the door. The men looked towards the door and saw Joel.

"Hey, I thought you guys were hungry. I made some chicken drumettes, sandwiches, stuff jalapenos, and some deviled eggs." She started moving around the room making and serving plates. When she got to the emotional ass nigga, he snatched the plate and threw it. I pulled her back and got in his face.

"I don't want that shit. I want the head of the muthafucker that took my brother."

Joel had her arms wrapped around my waist to calm me down. I knew that these niggas were going through it. But, what they won't do is take that shit out on Joel. "Calm yo mutha fucking ass down before I fuck you up. Clean this shit up and grab something else to eat." I told him.

Joel let me go and started picking up the mess. She passed him a plate and told him that she understood what he was going through. Everyone started eating and talking about other plans to take out the rest of Curtis' family. When we were done with Curtis' hoe ass, he wasn't going to have any family left. My parents came in along with Lilly. The conversation stopped about retaliation and we focused on more of the business aspects of the family.

Joel was talking to Ma and Lilly about going down south to see her brothers. I started towards them when Jordan walked up to me. "Jason, let me holla at you real quick."

I walked over to the bar where JJ was stuffing his face. Jordan turned towards me with a look I understood too well. He was about to ask me to do a job. A job I wasn't going to like. "Jason, I need you to find out who did this to Zeek. I promised his mom that I was going to take care of him. I can't tell that woman her other son isn't coming home without letting her know that we took care of it." Jordan said angrily.

I was about to tell him what I thought, but Joseph interrupted me. "Look, it was fucked up what they did to Zeek. I know you're mad and feel like this was your fault. On the other hand, we don't know what that nigga was into on the side. I mean, the nigga was in front them people house sitting. Before we start sending Jason on missions and shit, let's find out why he was killed." JJ said making sense. We always did that. Whatever I was thinking, he'd come out and say that shit. He knew that I couldn't express myself as much. He stepped in and took over, as a brother should. On the other hand, Jordan wasn't trying to hear that. He stared at JJ and gave him that 'don't fuck with me' look.

"Know your place JJ. I want the niggas that done this dead before midnight." He said to me still looking at JJ.

Joseph stepped up to him with his eyes blazing. "Don't send my brother out there on a guilt trip, bitch. If you want it done, you do it. Jason ain't doing that shit."

It was always like that with them two. Jordan was always pushing me beyond my limit. No matter how tough it was, he pushed, and I succeeded every rip. JJ didn't like that shit. He knew that I was out of control and that Jordan was using that to scare our enemies. I always did what Jordan asked of me. He was my big brother. But, as of lately, his orders have been questionable. I killed the Lewis' last week for coming up with some new ideas for territory equality. This nigga flashed out and told me to kill them all. I did it with no questions asked and, as I look back on it, the shit was foul.

I got in between them and stared Jordan in the eyes. I saw nothing but that darkness that covered me every single day. They shit flashed off and on when they were mad. My shit was constant. It lives through me every day. But Jordan telling Joseph to know his place, like he was some bitch, had me fuming. My father walked up mugging the fuck out of us. He hates it when we argue with each other.

"Whatever it is that got y'all mugging each other, you better cut that shit out. You will not do this in my house, with your mother in this room. Don't think because y'all grown, I can't fuck y'all up. Try me. Please do." My father said calmly, but very dangerously. It was in a whisper that you usually get when you're in public acting up with your parents. We were grown, true. But, when your father tells you to sit your ass down, you sit your ass down. We separated from each other without a backwards glance. The shit wasn't over. We just had to make it look that way.

I walked up to Joel and Mom, who didn't notice what happened between me and my brothers. They were talking about some other shit when I approached them. Not the one to beat around the bush about some shit I wanted to know, I asked. "When were you going to tell me about this trip of yours?"

She looked at me confusedly, like I didn't have that right to ask that shit. "Jason, I didn't think I was going anywhere until my brother called me. He has a business deal that needs my expertise. I'm leaving next week."

"Alright, you will stay here until it's time for you to leave. My boy G fixed your door already, but I will feel much better if you were here with me." I said, reaching for her hand. I had to touch her while I was in her presence. Something that I became addicted to now. She pressed her body closer to mine and whispered in my ear.

"Will you miss me?" She said before licking my earlobe.

She was lucky as fuck that my mom was standing in front of us. My mother knew about the potential threat that was put on the family. We needed for her to be aware of her surroundings when she left the house. Of course, she was going to be well-guarded, but you just didn't know what people were capable of these days.

"You know I will." I replied with a kiss on her forehead. She was breaking me down and didn't know it. I was feeling shit that I didn't expect to feel. It was new, but I didn't mind it now that it was for her. Shit, anything was better than the darkness that clouded my fucking head. My mother interrupted us with her nosey ass.

"So, Joel, how long will you be gone for?" She asked already knowing the answer. My mother was up to her usual shit. She was trying to tell me while Joel was gone, I needed to get my shit together. Because when she comes back home, she was going to be mine. No questions asked. I was ready to be in a relationship with Joel only.

"A week Ma-Ma. I just said that like two minutes ago." She said laughing at my mom. She knew what my mom was up to as well. She thought the shit was funny. If she only knew that shit was about to get real.

"Well, that should be enough time for both of y'all to get it together. Me and your father ain't getting any younger. We need some grandchildren running around here. I don't know what's holding Jordan and Lilly up. They been together for three years and still no kids. The fuck wrong with them? Maybe ya daddy need to give Jordan some fucking advice. Jordan Sr., put it on me so good, I got pregnant with two of y'all." My mother ranted. See what I'm talking about. I don't know what her and Joel be talking about. But, this shit right here, wasn't for me and Moms.

"Hold up! I don't want to hear nothing about you and Pops fucking." I walked off as they laughed at me. She was getting too damn comfortable with these conversations. I was going to have to tell Pops about this shit. He need to keep his wife under control. Loose mouth ass.

I looked around the once crowded room and saw that it was damn near empty. My Pops was talking to some of the crew members about some old school shit. I walked out the room to find my brothers. Lilly was fixing them to-go plates, while the other guys were eating the rest of the food that was put out.

I heard some arguing outside and knew that it was my brothers finishing up the discussion that our father interrupted. I walked out on the back patio and saw Jordan swing at JJ. JJ's head snapped to the left and stumbled a bit. Jordan always had a mean left hook. That shit was deadly. But, how JJ was still standing, you can tell that he didn't put his heart in that hit. JJ recovered and stared at Jordan. "So, that's what you do bitch? You swing on me because I disagree with the shit that is coming out of your mouth. You a hoe ass nigga fa that boy. But, if that's what you want. Let's do it then."

Jordan fucked up and he knows it. Not only did he lash out and take his anger out on family, but he just challenged JJ to a fight. JJ used to box when we were little. This nigga was a pure savage with fists that felt like iron. I should know. When we fought, he used to get in some good shots. I was smarter though and let him tire himself out, so that I can have the upper hand. The shit worked every time. Jordan never learned though and for that he was about to get some heavy hits from baby brother.

JJ walked up to Jordan with his set up, ready to take him down. I sat on the steps and prepared to watch the fight go down. I don't know what they were fighting for and I wasn't jumping in that shit either.

Jordan swung, JJ ducked and uppercut the fuck out of Jordan. Jordan fell clean on his ass. Usually, when shit like this happens, we would have stomped the fuck out of whoever we were fighting. But, Jordan was our brother. I would have to remind myself of that constantly when I was fighting them. Jordan got up dazed as shit. He shook it off and got ready for the blow to blow.

Before any of them could swing another punch, my mom came out there with her bat. I jumped off the steps and moved out her way. She didn't play with Matilda the Bat. She started swinging on JJ and Jordan. Them niggas looked hella funny dodging those swings. My mom was cursing their ass out. She hit JJ in the leg and Jordan in the arm.

"Alright Ma, we sorry. We not going to fight no more. Shit, Ma, put the bat down!" Jordan screamed rubbing on his arm. You would have thought that my mom played in *A League of Their Own*.

"Fa real, Ma, we were only playing. I promise." JJ said trying to calm my mother down. She was huffing and puffing.

"Let me tell you niggas something. You don't fight each other like that, you hear. When you were younger, me and your father let you two go at it to get that shit out of your system. As men, you should be able to talk shit out and handle it accordingly. The next time I see y'all like this again, I'm going to shoot you both." She said, what she said, and walked off. She looked at me and frowned. "You got something to say." She asked all fired up. I had several things to say but I wasn't saying that shit with that bat in her hand. I was smarter than them niggas.

"No Ma-Ma." I used the nickname Joel gave my mom. She walked past me and went back inside with the crew watching.

"Hey Jo, maybe we should send Ma after the niggas who killed Zee. She looks like she will fuck somebody up." One of the crew members said. Everyone laughed and went back to doing what they were doing. I walked up to my brothers and these niggas were still glaring at each other. Jordan turned my way and spoke.

"Find whoever did that to Zeek and take care of it. Let me know when it is done." He said that shit to me and walked off. JJ shook his head and rubbed his hand down his face roughly.

"Don't let Jordan send you on these blind ass missions, bruh." Joseph said to me.

"What happened to all of the other blind ass missions I was sent on. Nobody said nothing then. Why say something now when you know that this shit been going on." I said wondering why he was so vocal about the shit now. Jordan been on this power trip.

"I been feeling like this J. I told you this shit before nigga, but you never listen. Jordan see you slipping into the deep end bruh. You are treading that water and he ain't doing nothing but putting more weights on you. Tell that nigga no, that you need a break from all this shit. Why don't you go and take a vacation somewhere? You need to step away from this shit J, before we lose you." JJ slapped me on my shoulder and left me wondering what Jordan was up to.

TEN

JORDAN

I didn't know who JJ thought he was talking to, but he got the wrong nigga. I have been doing what I felt what was necessary to keep the family afloat. So, if we had to get rid of all them muthafuckers, that was something we had to do. I got the call from the Elites saying that Gage was going to be able to take out Curtis and the crew from Texas.

Now we had to find out what happened to Zeek. Joseph was right about that shit. I was feeling guilty about his death. Shit, I feel guilty about any of my crew members dying. Always wondering if the decisions I made caused them their deaths. My Pops talked to me about it, but the talk didn't help.

I needed Jason to handle this situation quickly. I wasn't used to sleeping with someone's death on my head like this. JJ called me selfish and a hoe. That's why he got that left. He didn't understand the position I was in. If we didn't retaliate, they were going to think that we were weak. I couldn't allow that. I left my parents' house with Lilly in the passenger's seat.

My baby had been quiet for a minute. When I came back from the hit, she said a few words to me. I thought she was giving me time because of the Zeek shit. But, even now, she hasn't talked to me. We came to the red light and I looked over at her. My baby girl was beautiful. She didn't deserve a nigga like me. I wasn't out here cheating on her or nothing like that. I just hated the fact that I couldn't promise her that I'd be home every night.

"Tell me what's on your mind Lilly." I asked her while taking her hand into mine. She turned my way to give me her undivided attention. I knew the shit was about to be serious. I saw the tears in her eyes and that shit had me pulling over. I parked at the Shell gas station and got out. I walked over to the passenger's side and opened the door. I grabbed her face and looked her in the eyes. "What's wrong Lilly? Tell me baby."

She took a deep breath and put her head down. I didn't allow that shit. Whatever it was she had to say, she was going to say it while looking at me. I was about to force her to look at me when she did it herself. "I think it will be best if I went by my parents for a while." She had the nerve to say. I looked at her like she grew three heads. She lost her fucking mind with this bullshit. She wasn't going anywhere.

"Fuck no. You got me fucked up thinking you gonna up and leave me. We gonna talk this shit out. Come up with some solutions and shit. You ain't leaving. So, don't bring this up again." I said grabbing her face tightly. "Do you understand me?"

I loved Lilly with everything in me. For her to think that leaving me was an option, had me losing my shit. She was supposed to be able to handle this shit. Why would she want to leave me after all the shit we been through? She wasn't taking my heart away from me. Nah, fuck that.

"I'm pregnant, Jo." She mumbled to me.

I stared at her and she was looking down again. She was nervous and trembling. I leaned in closer to make sure she said what I thought she said. "Say that again Lilly." I whispered gently. I didn't want her to think that I was unhappy with the news. Fuck, I was happy as shit. I was about to become a daddy.

"I'm pregnant, Jordan," she said a little louder than before.

"You look so beautiful right now, you know that." I kissed her lips and all over her face. "I love you so much, girl." I put my forehead against hers to calm myself down. I was ready to fuck her right here and now to make sure that she was carrying my baby. She went quiet again and that reminded me of her first statement. "Lilly, why do you want to leave, knowing you are pregnant with my baby?"

"It's a lot going on right now, Jo. I don't want to raise our baby alone because you out here in these streets. Jordan, I need you." She said crying. I didn't understand how my mom did it. But, there was no way I was going to let any potential threat loose. Not while my girl was carrying my seed. These hating ass niggas gotta die. If I had to do that shit myself, so be it.

ELEVEN

JASON

I woke up the next morning from another peaceful sleep. Joel stayed the rest of the week until it was time for her to visit her brothers. We talked about her life and mine. I wanted to get to know her more. I wasn't a fan of all this talking, but she made it easy. I told her about all the shit I went through and how I became the way I am. When I went to basic training, I got picked on because I was quiet and didn't fuck with nobody. My father warned me about my temper and how I should control it.

"Don't show them how mad you can get, but how calm you can be. That would scare the shit out of the average person." He told me this right before I took off. The shit worked for a little while until muthafuckers started to test me.

It was our final test before graduation. We had to complete several different scenarios as a team. I didn't work well with others, but I had to tolerate them to be a Seal. SR Turner and SR Brooks approached my rack talking shit. "Hey, don't fuck this up for us bitch. I worked too hard to let some punk like you get in the way of my goals. If you can't pull your weight let us know now." He told me getting too close.

"Get the fuck out of my face." I told him straight up. I didn't feel like doing this shit or dealing with these low self-esteem ass niggas. He was always around a group of people to carry him through. I turned my back, letting him know that I was finished with this conversation. He grabbed my arm to swing me around and I lost it. I hit that bitch in his throat. He dropped down to his knees and started gasping for air. I lifted my leg and kicked him in the middle of his face. I didn't care if he lived or died. I was prepared for the consequences of my action. Shit, I felt that I learned enough to become the better silent killer I wanted to be. My Chief Petty Officer Li pulled me to the side and told me to contain myself. He wanted me on the Seal team. I didn't get fucked with after that.

A knock on my door took me out of my trance. Joel walked in with a tray full of food. She had on one of those thin ass maxi dresses with a robe over it. This woman was going to have us all with high blood pressure and diabetes. I walked to the table that was in my room near the balcony window. She set the tray down and begin serving food to me. She wasn't doing it out of being obedient. She was doing it because of the nurturing tendencies that her mother drilled into her.

"What do you have planned today?" She asked me while cutting into her omelet. The spread was hefty. An omelet with veggies, meat, and cheese. Grits with salt and butter. No sugar peoples. Bacon, sausage, pancakes, hash, and a large glass of juice. She was going to have me sleeping after this. But, I had shit to do and people to kill.

"I received the phone call from my connect. He told me that he has information for me and need me to come over. Whatever it is, it can't be good for this fool to tell me to come to his house." I told her after I finished chewing my food. "It all depends on the information he gives me to determine my plans for the rest of the day. What are you doing today?"

"I will be going with Ma-Ma to her doctor's appointment since Pops will be attending a meeting with the Stand and Jordan." She told me. I was supposed to take Ma to her appointment, but I will have to ask JJ since my father will be accompanying Jordan to the meeting. "She wanted to do some shopping today. I told her that I would go because I need some things for my trip."

"That's cool. I will give you the money to get whatever you and my mom need. You better wear some flats too. She is going to have you in that mall all day buying unnecessary shit." I got up to take my wallet off my dresser. I took out my Black card and placed it on the table. She looked at me and then at the card.

"I don't want your money Jason. I'll give it to your mom, but I don't need it." She continued eating. I knew she didn't need my money. It was the principal though. I wanted to treat her the same way my father treated my mom, like a queen. I was about to tell her that but was interrupted by my phone. I picked it up and saw that it was Mya. I haven't seen her in two weeks. The last time I went over there, she gave me some head. My mind was so gone that I called out Joel's name. Mya didn't care. She kept going and addressed the shit after we were finished. She told me that she'd be whoever I needed her to be to stay in my life.

To me, that was a major turn-off. Women settled for anything because they didn't know their worth. I didn't do that side chick shit either. If the woman I was with couldn't be the only one, then she wasn't the one. These niggas were out here giving these hoes too much power. I told Mya no again flatly and made my exit. I haven't talked to her since.

I silenced the ringer and tossed my phone on the bed. I turned to go back to the table and it vibrated. I picked up and answered it this time. "What?"

"Hey, I haven't seen you in a while. Will I see you later tonight?" She ignored my attitude. She was used to it by now.

"No, you won't. I am in a relationship now. Don't call my phone again." I told her and hung up. There wasn't a reason to lead her on to think that we could be more. The one I wanted was sitting at the table staring at me.

"Who are you in a relationship with?" She asked with a smirk on her face. The games this woman played. She knew damn well who I was talking about. I walked to her and picked her up from her seat. I pushed the plates and tray aside to place her on the table. I sat down and spread her legs. I untied the robe and placed my hands on her thighs. I started caressing them while pushing her dress up. I kissed up her thighs until I reached black laced boy shorts. "I thought you knew the chick I was in a relationship with." I told her as her breathing picked up.

"No," she moaned out. She opened her legs even more to fit my broad shoulders.

I nudged my nose to her clit and the smell of her pussy had me starving. She jumped and moaned clutching my head. I licked her clit through her panties. She gripped my head tighter and moaned my name this time. That shit had me losing my shit. She was so responsive to my touch. I pulled back and was done with all the teasing. I had to get a taste of her sweet-smelling pussy. I took off her boy shorts and dived in that shit. I latched onto her clit. She started grinding on my tongue and I was enjoying it. I had my arms wrapped around her thighs pulling her closer to my face. I continued sucking on her clit and was trying to suck the soul out of her pussy.

"Oh, Jason, baby don't stop." She told me as her legs began to get tighter.

I didn't plan on it. I put two fingers in her gently and watched her facial expression change. Her mouth opened as if she wanted to scream but the shit was stuck in her throat. I moved my fingers in and out of her quickly. I wanted her to cum hard on my tongue. I felt her nub getting harder and her legs started trembling, as she bust in my mouth.

"Oh my, God, Jason." She screamed out. I knew my family heard her loud ass. I had to take her to my house to finish this shit up. She got my dick so hard right now. I licked my lips and was able to taste that sweet shit. My baby couldn't catch her breath to talk. She smiled down at me and shook her head.

"You still didn't answer my question." She had the audacity to say. That fucking mouth was going to get her in trouble, I swear.

"I'll answer that shit tonight." I said standing up and kissing her on the lips. If she would have turned away, I would have been pissed. If a woman couldn't taste herself then you know that she was fucked up below. Not my baby. She tongued me down. That shit had me about to fuck her on this table. I pulled back and adjusted myself. "I'm going to fuck you up for real."

"You promise." She asked licking her lips.

"I promise," I told her.

She smiled and climbed her ass off the table. We went into the bathroom to freshen up before going downstairs. I didn't want to kiss my mom with Joel's juices on my shit. We made it downstairs and my parents were talking about my mother's doctor's appointment. She was going in for her routine check-up. My grandmother and Aunt Cora died of breast cancer. The doctors caught their cancer when it was at stage five. We stayed on my mom about seeing her doctors faithfully. I wasn't going to lose her to no damn cancer.

"Call me as soon as you finish. We can go to lunch when I get out the meeting with the Stand. Hopefully, they can give us some information about what's going on." My father told my mom and kissed her. I was proud to say that my mother and father were happily married. Even through all the bullshit with the business, my mom stood by his side. That was the type of love I was wanting for myself. That shit that make you want to come straight home after a long day of work.

"I will. You guys just be careful, ok." She said to him.

"I gotta call Joseph over here to bring Ma to her appointment. My connect came through with some information. You would have to send Bruiser and Tank with them as well. Their crew will make sure she makes it there and back." My father nods at me. I turned around to Joel to give her instruction. "Look, you listen to whatever they tell you to do, with no questions asked. You understand? I don't want them fools calling me because your ass is out there being stubborn and shit."

"I know that the threat is real, Jason. I'll do my part and be good." She said too calmly for me. I don't know if she was being sarcastic or not. But, if anything happens to her or my mom out there, I was killing the crew whole family. On God.

"Aight, call me when you are done. Maybe we can have lunch with Ma and Pops." I said while reaching out to grab her. I kissed her softly but slapped her on that ass hard. She started cursing me out as I walked out the door. Oh well, I was going to be hearing a lot of that tonight. I jumped in my all black 2017 Monte Carlo SS and pulled off. I was playing the mix my baby made for me. She added some Pac, Nas, and Biggie to my shit. Have you ever been riding and listening to music that was so good, that you didn't want to get out of your car? I know I was driving slow as fuck on the interstate. I didn't care.

When I pulled up to this fool's house, I had to check the address again. Aaron was also on the Seal team with me, along with a nigga I became cool with named Sincere. He retired back to his hometown in New Orleans. He opened a karaoke bar and club called Magic Mic. The nigga was just like me in many ways, unlike Aaron.

The dude was smart as fuck. He was our computer geek for classified missions. He was able to find anybody that we were looking for in the middle of the jungle or the ocean. The house was a wide single home. It was tan with a big ass front yard. There were two cars in the driveway when I walked up to the front door. I knocked twice and stood on the side of the door. I hated standing in front of peepholes of any door.

Aaron opened the door and stepped to the side. I walked in and waited for him to lead the way. His house was dark on the inside. All the blinds were down and closed. He opened the door which had to be the basement. I reached the last step and looked back up. I felt like I was in an FBI office. He had monitors spread out across the wall and the table that sat in the middle of the floor. He had a big screen

TV on the back wall with the football game on. A huge ass bed was in the corner with a refrigerator across from it.

"What's up J?" He finally said after sitting down.

"Nothing, what's good with you Dex?" I asked him still staring at all this shit he had stored down here. They all had nicknames in our Seal crew. Aaron was called Dex because he reminded us of the little dude from Dexter Laboratory. He was short and medium built. He had pale skin, but tattoos were everywhere. I didn't have a nickname. I didn't want one.

"Let's get right to it, shall we? Curtis is living in Houston, Texas with his girlfriend Brandi Mitchell. Her family was killed a couple of weeks ago. That's his relation to this." He said pushing his glasses up on his face and typing on the keyboard.

"His ass is about to die trying to impress pussy." I replied shaking my head. This nigga knew he wasn't about this life. The call he made to Jordan was a bitch move.

"There's more. I checked to see who else was related to the Mitchells. Just in case you wanted to finish their family off on your own. The father had a sister that stay close to your brother Joseph. Eve Nicolas stays there with her three daughters and son. The daughters are Rachael, Roxanne, Riley and a son named..."

"Ricky," I interrupted furiously calm.

"Yep, he been going back and forth to Texas for a week now." He said as he typed on the keys. All the monitors were displaying pictures of him in airports here in Philly and in Texas. The other screen had his credit card transactions and phone records. "He has been calling Curtis for two weeks. When I found out who he was, I started following him and found this."

A screen came up with him being followed by Zeek. Ricky got out the car to approach Zeek's car and started loading off on him. Someone else jumped out the car to drive Zeek's car to the house. Now I know Zeek was down for us. We were going through all the calls when Ricky's phone began to ring.

"Tap into that." I told him.

"Like you had to ask." He said all smugly.

He connected to the call and we were able to hear the conversation.

"Please tell me you got at them niggas already." Curtis spoke.

"Nah, not yet. I'm following one of them right now. After I do this nigga in, I'm going to take out Jo and get Jason tonight." Ricky said with car horns blowing in the background.

"Who is the car with him?" Curtis asked.

"Their mother and the cook. I won't be leaving none of those muthafuckers alive." Ricky replied angrily.

"Good, make it happen." Curtis said and ended the phone call.

These bitches lost their fucking minds. I turned to walk off.

I got the information I needed to do what I needed to do. "Call if you need help, J." Dex said right before I reached the top step. I continued walking until I reached my car. I grabbed the handle and felt a burning sensation in my shoulder. Joseph. I reached for my phone and called my little brother. Phone went straight to voicemail.

"Fuck!" I yelled out before punching a hole through my window. I called Bruiser and he answered on the third ring. "My family," I asked feeling the change coming.

"They are good. Ms. Joyce alright and Joel is driving. Joseph got hit near the chest, but he is still conscious." I hung up the phone and noticed how numb I was becoming. I took a deep breath and let the darkness consume me.

TWELVE

JORDAN

I knew that the meeting wouldn't go my way. I was demanding more territory from all the members. It was only right that we had more. Our family was bringing in more merchandise and taking all of the risks. No one would have been able to link anything back to us. It was just the principle. My father of course disagreed. He said that I was being greedy and causing a rift between the families. He just didn't see my vision. But, it was all good. Whoever didn't comply, was going to get a visit from Jason. No bullshit.

My phone rang and it was Joseph calling. "Hey, how was Mom's doctor's appointment?" I asked him while putting him on speakerphone.

"We got hit! The muthafuckers tried to take out my mom nigga. We are killing these bitches on sight. Anybody that fuck with this nigga back then and now, is getting it. I want the bitch that taught him how to read and all. Fuck!" JJ screamed out in pain. I slammed my feet on the gas and headed to the safe house.

I couldn't talk, but I had to ask. "How is Ma, JJ? Tell me that Ma is okay." I asked nervously. I killed many along with my brothers. I couldn't prepare for a loss like this. My Pops looked at me waiting for the answer. My brother got quiet and the noise in the background got louder.

"Hey you guys. Ma-Ma is fine. We all are except Joseph. He was hit in the shoulder while driving us home. We will tell you guys about it when you reach the home. I already called Lilly and told her to come here. Tank will meet her. Just make it safe." Joel's voice came through the speaker and then hung up.

My father became anxious and started fidgeting with his keys. "Don't worry, Pops, everyone is good. Ma is safe, and you know that JJ will be alright." I tried to ease his mind. I know that it was going in overdrive.

"In all the years that I have been the boss in this family, your mother has never been the target. Not. Once. If I were you, I would get this shit under control and quick. Because if I step in, you will be sorry." My father said to me. That shit sent chills down my spine. I have never been on my dad's bad side. I will have to get this shit handles asap.

I pulled up to the house out in Chester. A two-story house, with four bedrooms and three baths. It was white and stormy grey. There wasn't much furniture in there. We barely used it for anything. Like my father said, we never had trouble like this. My pops jumped out the car before I put that bitch in park. I got out the car and ran up the stairs behind him. They had seven guys guarding the front door. We walked in and you can hear JJ cursing about the pain he was feeling. Pops made it to where they were and grabbed my mother into a bear hug.

"You are not to leave my side again Joyce. Wherever you go, I go. I don't want to hear no shit." He said to her while checking for damages at the same time.

"I'm alright Senior. Joel covered me with her body. She pulled me from my seat and she told me to get on the floor of the car. My babies did good." She was referring to JJ and Joel.

"Thank you, Joel. I am happy to see that you are ok as well." He told her. He pulled her into a hug and kissed her on the forehead.

Pops told her thanks again before walking over to Joseph. He grabbed the back of Joseph's neck. Pops leaned his head to the top of his and whispered something for JJ's ears only. JJ nodded his head and bump fists with Pops.

"Tell us what happened." Pops asked and took a seat with mom on his lap.

"We were on our way to the fresh market to get some things for lunch. Ma didn't want to be eating out, knowing that we had problems. I was on Joshua Rd and Germantown Pike when the cars started rushing us. I hit the gas and made that left. I had a car on each side of me. Bruiser was in front of us and Tank was in the back. I was shooting out the window, but the crew took them out. I got hit and swerved onto the shoulder, and Joel came from the back to drive, when everything was clear. I came here and called you guys." Joseph painfully spoke.

The bullet was too close to his chest for my comfort. I turned and looked at Lilly walking in. She saw the blood on JJ and ran straight to the bathroom. I went to check on her. She had been having all day sickness. I knew seeing all that blood turned her stomach out. I walked into the bathroom and she was dry heaving over the toilet. I sat on the toilet and rubbed her back. "Is he alright." She asked me after she was done.

"Yeah, baby. They all are okay." I told her still rubbing her back. I helped her up and walked her to the bathroom sink. She used the mouthwash and splashed her face with water. "I quit my job today. I felt that it was unsafe for the children to have someone like me in the school." She said with sadness. I didn't know how I felt about that. It's true that I wanted her to quit, but not like this.

"Baby, we can work something out and get your job back." I said to her. I was going through different ways in my mind to get her back to feeling secure at her job. I knew that if anything would have happened to them kids, she would have blamed herself. I would never forgive myself for putting her in that position. She interrupted my thoughts with her hands on my face.

"Don't worry about it, Jordan. We will have our own for me to teach. Starting with this one." She said as she removed her hand from my face. She then placed them on her flat stomach. That made me smile and worry. They were already after my mom and Joel. I knew that this nigga was going to send someone after Lilly. I grabbed her and held on tightly. It started tonight.

I walked back out with Lilly in tow. She went to my mother's open arms and cried. Joel rubbed her back to calm her. My father shook his head and walked up to her. He pulled her out my mother's arms and stared at her. My mother and Joel were smiling at the two.

"Since my son don't have the nuts I gave him to tell me himself. Maybe you can be the sweet young lady I know you are and tell me yourself." He told her with a goofy ass smile on his face. She smiled up to my father like he was her own.

"You are going to be a grandfather." She said quietly. My father picked her up and swung her around. Joseph, completely forgetting that he got shot, jumped up and pushed me.

"This why you been tripping Jo. The whole time you been doing this because Lilly was pregnant, and you weren't going to tell us." He asked angrily. I didn't know what to tell him. I mean this was one of the reasons why I was on a hundred today. I had my own agenda before Lilly came in the picture. I wanted everything to be ours. The baby just enhanced my drive.

"Yeah Nigga. I was going to tell y'all after this shit died down." I told him. He pulled me in a hug and patted me on my back. "Well, then, I'm in Jo. Whatever your plan is, I'm in."

"Thank you, Jesus! You know how long I've been praying for this." My mother said grabbing Lilly and Joel's hand. "Come on, it's time to go home and feed my baby. She needs her rest carrying that child. Lilly, all Jordan did was kick the shit out of me when he was in my stomach. When I ate, he was just as calm as can be."

"Wait Ma, we have to be careful. We don't know if them niggas followed y'all back here or waiting for us to go to the house." I told her. They hear baby news and forget everything that is going on with the family.

"Joseph left Jason a message about what was going on. We have some hard hitters with us right now. Trust me when I say that we will be alright." She smiled at me like she knew something that we didn't know.

"Let me find out you got a secret weapon, old lady." Joseph said walking in front her. She reached out and slapped the shit out of him.

"You keep fucking with me and I lay your ass out." She told him and walked past him mumbling about how she didn't give a shit about him getting shot. He was making faces behind her back. My father came from behind him and slapped him again.

"Don't play with my wife, boy."

I started laughing. This fool never learned.

It was after ten when we got to the house. Mom and Dad wanted to stop at every store that had baby shit. They were acting all freely and shit. I turned to tell JJ something and this bitch was pushing a stroller.

"My nephew is going to like this shit." He said smiling. You couldn't tell that this nigga just got shot a couple of hours ago. I think it was those happy pills Joel had in her purse.

We were carrying shopping bags in, when the crew pulled up. Brian came rushing up to us with tears in his eyes. The women went inside while we stayed back to see what happened.

"They got Rick, man. Somebody killed the whole family." Brian said distraught.

JJ and Brian were the Godfathers of Rick's baby girl Saniya. I know this nigga was crying more over her than Rick. I didn't want to know the details of their death. I just needed to know why. He was already acting suspiciously. It was only right to get what he deserved, but not the baby. She didn't have anything to do with what was going on.

JJ stepped up to Brian and asked what he saw. "Blood, man. There was blood everywhere. They were stabbed multiple times.

What was crazy about the whole scene was their eyes were looking at Rick."

"Their bodies were facing Ricks." JJ asked getting angry.

"No, Nigga. He cut their eyes out and had them surrounding his body. The shit looked like something you see in the movies." He said breathing hard. "What type of crazy muthafucker would do something like that?"

"Look, let's go into the office and talk about this some more. I will call Jason and see if he can use his connections." I said.

We all walked into the house and headed towards the office. The men passed the women and spoke to them. Joel promised dinner like always and headed to the kitchen. When I opened the door, the sight before me put me on pause.

THIRTEEN

RICK

Sorry to interrupt your story, but I got some shit to say. Yeah, it was me. I was trying to kill them all. Ms. Joyce never done anything to me. Jordan said it best though. Take out the muthafuckers that birth such arrogant ass niggas. She knew that these niggas weren't wrapped too tight. Mr. Jo and Ms. Joyce put them on some type of pedestal that made them think that they could look down on others.

At first, we were cool. Anything that they had, they shared with the crew. But, it was nothing like your own. Call me selfish all you want. I had to do what was necessary for my family to shine just like the Davis crew. My mother moved from Texas with the rest of us. She was trying to get away from that life my uncles had. She didn't want to be a part of something that would put us in danger. I understood where she was going with her plans. It just wasn't meant for a nigga like me. This shit was in my blood. I couldn't escape this shit if I wanted to.

JJ put me on with the Davis crew. He told me that I was his right-hand. I knew that shit wasn't true. He had two brothers that I knew wouldn't let that shit happen. Jason was always watching a nigga. I had to wait for that clown to leave to put my plan into action.

I was going to take the Davis crew out. I wasn't bringing anybody on. Shit, I barely trusted myself. I knew that I wasn't loyal to them niggas and played that shit well. I didn't need no make-believe ass niggas around me. I guess Zeek caught on and tried to check me about some shit that wasn't his business. I hit his ass with twelve rounds and put him in front Curtis' people's house.

Curtis thought that I was doing this for my cousin and that we were going to run this shit together. He just didn't know. After I finished with the Davis crew, I was flying up there to deal with the rest of his crew. I was tired of eating out of another muthafucker's hand. It was time for me to stand on my own.

Shit went left quick with the hit on JJ. I waited at the intersection for them to come through. I told one of the guys that Jason wanted me to tag along with them. He texted me to let me know what road they were on and where they were going. When we saw the three black Escalades, we started the car and went straight at them. Of course, y'all know I missed the hit on their mom.

Now I was at home packing to get the fuck out of dodge. I had to let shit cool down before going on with the rest of the plans. I was headed to Texas with my girl and our four-year-old daughter Saniya. My mother was coming along just for the trip. I was going to call JJ and tell him that Curtis sent his boys after my family. He had no choice but to believe that shit.

"Hey, we are about to pull out in a minute. Make sure you got what you need." I yelled out to them. I picked up my bag and started walking down the stairs. The door was wide open. I went to put my bags in the car and noticed that my bags were the only ones in there. I remembered Brittany telling me that their bags were in the car. I went back into the house and closed the door. She was going to make a nigga bat the fuck out of her.

"Hey Brit, where the fucking bags at." I yelled for her. I was headed back upstairs when I heard some clicking noise. I took a step back and walked towards the family room. I really didn't have time for the games right now. "Man, let's go before you get left." I hollered walking in the room.

I closed my eyes and opened them back up to see if this was a nightmare or real life. "This shit can't be real." I kept repeating to myself. My daughter, mother, and Brittany were stretched out on the floor. I knew this nigga was crazy, but not this crazy. All of them had stab wounds all over their body. There was blood spatter everywhere. Brittany and my mother were missing their eyes. They looked like they struggled right up to their last breath. My baby girl didn't fight. She couldn't. She was only a baby.

What the fuck did she have to do with this? I dropped down to my knees and crawled to my baby. I screamed and cried with everything that was in me. I looked over to my mom and cried harder. I put her in this position. I can't tell her how sorry I was and how I was going to make things better. Brittany had tears and blood running down her face. I tried to grab all three, but it was hard. No one would ever know how this felt.

I looked up into the eyes of a soulless man. I heard the stories about this nigga, but I never seen it for myself. He was smirking and rocking in the chair. I stood up to my feet. Not caring at this point if I lived or died. Jason was sitting in the rocking chair, feeding off my agony. He was wearing the blood of the most important people in my life. He was tapping a big ass knife on the coffee table.

I knew that luck was what I needed to get past this nigga. It should be easier to take him out while he was sitting. I took a step towards him and something shiny was thrown at me. It was another knife that landed in the wall over my head. I didn't see him move at all. I looked around for more people and the bitch started laughing at me. I didn't find nothing funny at this moment. I tried to rush him with my eyes directly on him. He moved and punched me on the side of my head. I fell face first in my mother's blood. I got up and fell right back down.

I wasn't going to be an easy kill for this nigga. Naw. I got up and wiped the blood from my face. "Come on J. Do you really need a weapon to kill me? Big bad ass Jason. Come on nigga, let's go work. Man to man." I started baiting him in. JJ and I used to box when were younger. Me and JJ was what and what in boxing and JJ told that, he used to whip Jason ass. If Jason couldn't beat JJ, I knew that my chance of winning would be greater.

He placed the knife on the table and removed his shirt. I removed mine as well. I looked down at the women in my life and let the rage take over me. I charged at Jason with rage and determination. I hit him with body shots and then one to the head. He didn't block the punches. He took them in and countered with another blow to my head. I was dizzy but didn't let that slow me down. I was still hitting him and thought I had a chance to win until I slipped.

Right away, I put my hands over my head to block the feet I knew were coming. When there weren't any, I looked up and saw Jason giving me time to get up. Without wasting another minute, I got up and went at him again. He hit me with that Popeye's special. One to the mouth and the other to the nose. I fell again and didn't have time to cover up. That nigga put his knee in my chest and started punching me in the face over and over. I turned my head to look at my daughter.

I love you Saniya. Daddy sorry baby. That was the last thing I remembered because that nigga's final blow took me out.

FOURTEEN

JASON

I sat and waited for my next victims in the dark. Blood was dripping from my knuckles and my face. I was high as fuck on them kills and I needed more. The shit I found out at Rick's house had me seeing more than red. I didn't want to do this, but it was law around here.

I heard the voices coming towards the office. The door opened, and this paper mache ass nigga walked in. I can't believe that me and this nigga had the same blood running through us. I used to look up to this clown. I wanted to make him proud of me and do the shit he asked me to do, with no problems. Here it is, this nigga was playing us all. I was staring through this nigga's soul and that shit was grimy. He was looking at me, hoping that I didn't figure his punk ass out.

I felt more than saw Joseph walking towards me. I didn't make eye contact with him. I just let the anger seep through, so that he could feel that shit. He stopped midstride.

"Jason," he said in a cautious voice. He felt my anger and where it was directed.

I shook my head to let him know that they can't get out of this. He took a step back and looked at Jordan. They made eye contact and held their own conversation. Jordan looked back at me with wide eyes. Yeah muthafucker, I see you, nigga.

My father walked in and my eyes went to him. He was the one that birthed this nigga. We had a set law. Take out the ones that made these hoe ass niggas. My father, a man that I respected more than myself, was the reason that nigga was breathing. He had to go too. I got ready to stand up when my mother walked in.

"Jason, where is my son." My father asked softly.

I ignored him and continued holding eye contact with my mother. My fucking heart. I knew she didn't raise his ass to be what he was today. Shit, JJ and I was nothing like his stupid ass. We always went the way Pops told us. He knew the ins and outs of the game. What Jordan got out of it, who knows? But, there were no exceptions.

I looked in the eyes of all the mothers and fathers I murdered. I knew that some of them didn't have anything to do with how their children turned out. They still had to die because of what their offspring did. What made my parents so different? I knew that Jordan's actions were going to lead this family into the grave. Before I let that happen, I'll take them all out myself.

My mother was about to walk to me when Pops and JJ pulled her back.

"Let me go. My baby needs me." She told them while struggling in their arms.

"That's not your son, Joyce. That's not our boy." My father spoke sadly.

He knew what I was thinking. They all knew that it was going to take more than a couple of bullets to get me down too. I stood up and everyone behind my family stood back. JJ and Jordan stepped in front of my parents. I'll make JJ's shit quick, but that bitch Jordan was going to suffer. I let the darkness consume me even more to continue with my plan. I smiled at Jordan with the blood of Ricky and his family still running down my face. That nigga looked sorry, but the shit wasn't enough.

I was walking towards them when Joel walked in. My eyes were automatically drawn to hers. It was something in those beautiful eyes that couldn't be trusted. Something was there in her eyes that I couldn't decipher. When I was usually in this state, I was able to see everything. Joel was closed off for some reason. She had sandwiches and shit in her hands. She handed the tray to one of the guys without breaking eye contact. Joel stared and then started towards me. Joseph tried to grab her arm, but she snatched it from him. He tried again and stumbled back from the look in her eyes. Pussy.

She turned towards me with those same eyes. The same eyes I used to stare at before we went to bed were gone. Her eyes were as dark as mine. Before I knew it, she was standing in front of me with her hands up. She was showing me that she was no harm to me. I didn't know why she would think that. I shook my head and her eyes got softer. She was telling me to trust her. Understanding. Compassion. True loyalty is what she was displaying in her eyes.

She raised her hand to touch me and I frowned down at her. "Don't fucking touch me." I said deeper than my original voice.

Joel looked at me like I was a disobedient child. Her eyes went back dark, and she frowned. Her hand came closer to my face again until they were on my temple. She rubbed and caressed me. I was like a demon being pet by my maker. I grabbed her by the waist and picked her up. I squeezed her tightly and didn't want to let her go. I put my head on her chest and listened to how calm her heart was beating.

"I know Jason. I know." She repeated to me over and over. I pulled back to look at her. "Let me take care of you, Jason. Let's go baby." She said softly but with meaning behind it. I stared at her. She was looking straight through me. I put her down and followed her towards the door. I looked back at Jordan with a warning. Because if Joel couldn't bring my high down, I was coming back for all of them.

I followed her out the back door. She was walking me to the pool house out back. Good. I didn't want any interruptions. I knew that, after witnessing my mood, my brothers left to put my parents into hiding. We approached the door and slid it open. There was a Cuetec pool table to the left of us and a large black sectional to the right. The sectional faced the multiple sliding doors. The kitchen matched the black and white décor with a custom-made breakfast bar. The two bedrooms and baths were towards the back.

Joel dropped my hand to close the open blinds and curtains. She turned around with eyes blazing. Blood was on her clothes and all over the side of her face. I took her hand and dragged her to the bathroom. I pushed the door opened and slammed her to the wall. She was beautiful to me.

I raised my hand to rub her face and noticed that my hands were still covered in blood. I ripped her clothes and tossed them behind me. I reached into the walk-in shower and turned the water on hot. Before I could tell her, Joel walked in without flinching. She put her head underneath the waterfall shower head and motioned for me to come in. I kicked off my shoes and pulled down my jeans with my boxer briefs.

I walked in and joined her in the shower. The scolding water felt good on my body. Joel looked to be enjoying it as well. She grabbed the sponge and started cleaning the blood off my body. I wanted to clean her, though. I didn't want that nigga's blood all over her. I snatched the sponge from her and started scrubbing her body. I didn't want to hurt her, but this shit had to come off. She turned and obeyed me without me asking.

She picked up some vanilla smelling shit and placed it on the sponge. The scent itself was soothing, but I was ready to get out. I took a quick shower and stepped out. I took the towel that was hanging on the rack and pulled Joel out the shower. I gave her the towel and walked towards the bedroom without drying off. When we got there, I turned to see that she was still wet.

Cold eyes again. She walked around me as she was surveying her prey. I never thought of myself that way, especially in the bedroom. She stopped in front of me and waited for instructions. "Get in the bed, Joel." My voice sounded raspy. I never heard myself speak in this state.

She climbed into the bed still wet from the shower. She had put a dip in her back which had her ass up. I walked towards her and bit both her ass cheeks. I was feeling like I was deprived of this. She moaned my name out. She looked back at me with her bottom lip between her teeth. Joel started shaking her ass begging for me to slap it and I gave it to her. I hit her so hard that my hand was stinging. I looked down and saw my baby girl dripping that good shit.

My baby was getting off on the pain. I wanted to taste her badly, but my dick couldn't wait. He was about to walk up in that pussy on his own. I grabbed her hips and pushed into her.

"Fuuuck!" I groaned. Never had a woman had me speaking during sex. Joel didn't wait to adjust to shit. I felt myself stretching her shit out. She was nice, warm and wet. She started throwing that shit back at m like she was possess. I pulled out to regain control. Joel jumped up and faced me with a frown on her face.

"Get your ass back in position. I didn't tell you to fucking move." I pushed her back down aggressively and slammed back into her pussy. She was moaning and shaking her ass on my dick. This shit was new to me. Women screamed and yelled out in pain from the fucking I was gave them. Joel was taking this shit and throwing it back with force.

I pulled out two more times, before I said fuck it, and busted all in her shit. I looked at the time and saw that we were going at this for almost two hours. Joel turned and looked at me. She was still biting her lip which had my dick getting hard again.

"My turn." She said getting up.

I sat down and leaned back to watch what she had in store for me. She dropped to her knees and swallowed my dick. I felt her tongue rotating around my shit. I grabbed her hair to make her go deeper. She slapped my hand away and did it on her own. My baby was sucking all the life out of my dick.

"You got that, bae. Suck that shit, El."

She moaned, and I felt that shit through my body. I pulled her head away before I spilled my seeds into her mouth. She licked her lips and climbed on top of me. Joel pushed me back and sat up. She was squatting over my dick while maintaining eye contact. I felt the heat from her pussy before it touched the tip of my dick.

Joel slowly sat on it until I was all the way in. She closed her eyes and her head fell back. She started moving up and down slowly at first. Her pussy felt like it was throbbing around my dick. She placed her finger on her clit and went wild from there. I tried to grab her, but she wasn't having it. I popped her ass and grabbed her waist.

"Stop fucking playing with me." I told her.

I didn't know what the fuck she thought it was. I pushed her back and forth, stroking up to meet hers. "Harder J, make this pussy cum." She demanded of me. I sat up and went to the edge of the bed. She wrapped her legs around me and fell back. This shit had me going deeper inside her. I pulled her body to me faster and harder.

"Yes, J. Don't hold back, I can take it." She told me. I got up slightly, with my legs still bent and went deeper. After four more strokes, we were both moaning out our orgasm. I fell back on the bed and pulled her up with me. She rested her head on my chest and fell asleep. I was behind her with a clear mind.

FIFTEEN

JORDAN

"Mom, let's go. We don't know what will happen when he comes out. I don't want you or Pops here when he gets out." I told my mom pushing her out the door with my Pops. I don't know what that nigga was going through to threaten the family. Clearly, this nigga was too far gone to see us as that.

I caught his warning loud and clear, though. I wasn't afraid for myself, but for my family, yes. Lilly was eleven weeks pregnant. I don't know if Jason had that information. Just in case, she will be leaving with them as well. When they are off the grid, I will confront this shit with Jason myself.

"Jordan, what is it that you are not telling me? My boy wouldn't look at us this way for nothing. Tell me what is going on now. Do it have anything to do with the demands that were made at the meeting?" My father asked. I couldn't tell him much. I just wanted to get them out of here before it was too late.

"Pops, I will explain everything. I need you to leave right now." I told him eagerly. We all were looking around each other to see if this nigga was going to pop up. Joel must have had this nigga occupied. He didn't miss an opportunity to kill anyone. The look she gave

Joseph had me stepping back on the slick. She had walked up to Jason like she created the killer in him. The calmness that he used to get from our mother couldn't help us at all.

"Where is Jason now?" Lilly asked me while shaking.

"Baby, you guys leave. I will talk to you later baby." I told her. I kissed her goodbye and walked them to the car.

"Have your ass at the house after you find out whatever triggered that shit in him." My mother finally said. She was quiet ever since Joel removed Jason from the room. You can tell that she was hurt by what she saw. Her baby covered in someone's else blood. The shit freaked us all out. I had seen this nigga killed many without a care in the world, but nothing like this though.

"I will Ma, go." I told her. They all got into the truck with Bruiser and Tank. The two wouldn't be enough to stop Jason, but they would slow him down for back up.

When the truck pulled off, I signaled the men to surround the pool house. Jeff stopped and looked at me. "Man, I'm not doing this shit. That is Jason in there no matter what you see right now." I ignored him and walked back into the house. Joseph was still in the office. He was in pure disbelief of what we witnessed. My phone beeped, and it was my connect. The message was a go for my plan. I had to push it back a little more to take care of this shit. I walked into the office looking down on my phone. I replied, "not now" and looked at JJ. He was sitting at the bar in a daze.

"I have never seen my baby brother like that, bruh. It was as if he was looking straight through us. For a minute, I was his enemy. He would have killed us, Jordan. I felt the hate and anger that was directed at us. What the fuck happened?" He asked me. I didn't know what to tell him. I was trying to find out who blood was all over him.

"Look, we gotta have a plan for when he comes out, JJ." I told him.

"Bitch, what are you talking about? I am not killing my fucking brother. He is lost, man. Anybody could see that shit. Nah, I'm going to try to talk to him." JJ said sounding all kinds of stupid.

"Nigga, did you see the same muthafucker I'm referring to? That was not Jason. If we don't do something about this shit right now, he will kill Ma and Pops." I told him yelling at this point. I loved my brother, but that nigga was at a point of no return. Jason wasn't taking my parents from me without a fight.

"Go ahead, Jo. I'll take care of Jason myself." Joseph looked up to me and said. "Go and protect Ma and Pops. Make sure Lilly get some rest too. She can't be stressing out over you while pregnant and shit."

"I'm not leaving you here by yourself." I stood in front of him.

"You don't have a choice Jo. Do it now, bruh. Take the crew with you. Because if any of them niggas slip and shoot my brother, I will kill them all. On God." He said meaning every word.

My phone started ringing with Lilly's face appearing. I knew that she was worried and that she was in a critical time in her pregnancy. "Go Jo." JJ told me while he lit one of his cigars.

I pulled that nigga in a hug and told him I love him. "Call me as soon as you leave from here. Do you understand me?" I told him. If anything happens to JJ, Jason was going to die for real.

I walked out the office and went to the back of the house. I called Brian and told him to leave with the crew. Jeff was guarding the door to make sure none of them niggas went in after Jason. I got in the car and headed towards the other safe house. Me and my father was about to have a talk that I knew was going to have him looking at me in a different way. He told me to run the family how I saw fit. My vision for the Davis crew was already in motion without any breaks.

SIXTEEN

JASON

I woke up relaxed and in a peaceful mood. Joel had to leave early to catch her flight to see her brother. She asked me to behave until she got back. I smiled at her and told her to get back to me quick. I needed her here with me to keep me sane. I found out a lot of shit that couldn't be ignored. I sat up and saw the breakfast on the table. I couldn't do nothing but shake my head. I don't remember when she prepared this for me, but I was thankful.

I went to the bathroom to take care of my hygiene. I came back out and attacked my loaded omelet with toast and bacon. I drank the juice and got up to take my dirty dishes to the kitchen. As I walked from the back, I heard someone in the kitchen. I knew it wasn't Jordan's punk ass. My Pops was not going to leave my mother's side. I wasn't that cool with the niggas in the crew but Jeff. I know that his ass wasn't in here eating the food that my baby cooked for me. I stopped near the kitchen and felt the worries of my lil brother. I took a deep breath before continuing into the kitchen.

Joseph was eating with his head down. He was mad at me. Pissed even. He will soon understand why I went from zero to a hundred. I placed my plate in the sink and turned to face my brother. He was staring back at me now. He pushed his plate to the side and stood up. He walked around the breakfast bar and got in my face. I knew what was coming next. Me and Joseph felt more like twins than anything. I felt his emotions from where I was standing. He was disappointed in me. And that was something that I wasn't used to. Not from my baby brother.

I had all the time in the world to prepare myself for it, but he needed this. JJ gut punched me then grabbed me by my throat and forced me to look at him.

"If you ever look or think the shit you were thinking about my mother and father again, I will forget that we are brothers and kill you, nigga." He said and shoved me away from him. He walked away and sat back at the breakfast bar. "Tell me what you know." He asked as he continued eating like he didn't just hem me up on the kitchen sink.

I knew he was hurting and needed to get that out of his system, so that we can move forward. I gave him that free one and ignored the urge to slap the fuck out of him. I leaned back into the sink and didn't know where to start. I looked him in the eyes and began telling him what I thought that he should know about his brother.

"Jordan sent them people at DJ. He was trying to find a way to take Derrick Sr. out without getting his hands dirty. He sent Rick and Zeek to Texas to meet up with the Mitchells. Rick volunteered because he wanted to visit his people. That whole time, that nigga, Rick, was plotting on us as well. He was in the truck busting at y'all. He wanted to kill us because he wanted to be the king of the Davis crew. This bitch wasn't a fucking Davis and thought that he should have been sitting at the table with you and Jordan. Rick took the information from Jordan to gain some of the alliances to take us out."

I let Joseph take in all the shit that I was saying to him. I knew that he was the Godfather of Rick's baby. So, my next words were going to be tough for him. "My contact gave me the information that Rick was trying to kill Ma. I went to his house and done the family in. I made it quick, JJ. Baby girl didn't suffer."

"Fuck, J! You think that shit make me feel better. Saniya had nothing to do with that. She was just a child." JJ spat at me angrily after throwing his plate to the wall. That nigga was trying not to put his hands on me fa real that time. I heard his knuckles cracking after he balled up his fist. "She was innocent in all this. You could have let her go Jason. I mean, are you that fucked up that you don't know the difference between the innocent and the guilty?

"So were the others, JJ. All of the other parents and kids were innocent too." I told him. He knew that Rick was into some other type of shit. He couldn't live after that. "That's not all. Jordan is planning to take the Stand out. All the fathers and first-born sons. He wants to run the Stand on his own. I killed Greg and Sean two months ago. He told me that it was about some territorial shit. I got my connect looking into that now. Rick and Zeek took out Chris and David at the club downtown. Zeek caught on to what Rick was planning and planned on telling Jo, but Rick got to him first and put his car in front of Curtis people house."

"Wait, nigga. That's a lot of shit to take in." He said taking a seat. "Ok, that shit with Rick and Zeek is all the way fucked up. Zeek was already too young for this shit. Jordan told me that someone sent the assassins after Greg and Sean. And the shit with Chris and David was said to be a set-up with the dude they jumped a few weeks back." He said in disbelief.

"Nah, I killed them both on the day DJ was kidnapped." I told him. He sat and took in all the shit that I was saying. He knew what the next step had to be. Jordan had to go. Brother or not, he was doing some fuck boy shit.

"That nigga lied to me like that. He told me it was because Lilly was pregnant." JJ told me while walking into the kitchen. I took a good look at him. This nigga had on the same bloody clothes from yesterday. He had bandages and shit on his chest. He was tired and worried. I felt that shit through my body. JJ was carrying so much weight around. I wasn't going to make him choose between me and Jordan. That was some hoe shit to do. But, I already made up my mind. I wasn't killing for this family until they were under some new management.

"How are you feeling?" I asked him anyway.

"I don't know what to feel man." He said tiredly.

"You saw Joel this morning." I asked him while picking up the glass from the plate he threw. I walked back to the breakfast bar and threw the glass away. I made me some juice and started drinking.

"Yeah, she told me to come in and eat some breakfast, take a shower, and carry my ass to bed. I told her that I was waiting on you to wake up." He started shaking his head. "Ya girl told me if I touched you, it was going to be a problem. Sad part about that is, I believed her. The way Joel looked at me last night had a nigga low-key scared for a minute. She the one for you, nigga. Ain't no way CH CH CH Jason was going to let us out there alive. She came up big for the fam."

I started choking on the juice that I was drinking. "What the fuck did you just call me?"

"CH CH CH Jason. I was looking for you to have a machete in your hand. You were already dressed in blood." Joseph said it casually. I never knew what I looked like when I became that Jason. Don't get me wrong, I still have control over myself. I just didn't care. That's what the military teaches you. When you are on the battle-field, it is you or them. When coming up against me, it was always them.

"I'm about to go get some rest and a shower. Jordan should be coming back over here when I didn't call or text him back." He started walking towards the other bedroom in the back. He stopped and let out a frustrated sigh. "Don't kill him yet, J. Let's find out where his mind has gone to. He fell off somewhere and, as his brothers, we have to put that nigga back on track. That's what family do. We make mistakes, we forgive each other, and then move the fuck on."

"Fuck that, JJ. When he is in the position that he is in, he can't make mistakes like that. If he was so concerned about family, he wouldn't have put us in the position that we are in. He can't lead for shit. Hell, I wouldn't follow him to the corner and back."

"For Ma, Jason. Do it for Ma. You owe her that for last night." He told me seriously.

I thought about it a bit before nodding my head. I really didn't want to talk or see my parents after last night. I didn't know how they felt about me now that they have witnessed who their son really was. My brothers' and Pop's faces were priceless. Mom looked angry. She didn't show fear, like the others did. She looked like she was ready to take out a muthafucker just for pushing me to the edge. I don't know what to do next. For the first time in life, I didn't follow through with my targets. I shook my head in disgust when I heard my phone ringing in the bedroom. I went to the back to retrieve it and saw that it was Joel. Baby girl be right on time fa real.

"Are you on your way back yet?" I asked her seriously. She had my head gone on how she handled me last night. I was craving for her shit like a crackhead. She had been gone for four hours and the shit felt like twenty-four.

"No, not yet. I just called to tell you that everything is going to be alright. Stop thinking so hard, nigga. I know you probably driving Joseph up the wall with that shit." She said laughing.

"How do you know what I was thinking about?" I asked her.

"Because, I know you Jason. Ma-Ma and Pops will forgive you. They know their son and what he is capable of. They know that you didn't just wake up wanting to kill them. You have triggers, baby. Those triggers have been hit. Let Pops know so that y'all can work that shit out. Ma-Ma already knows. Trust me." She said with so much understanding.

"How long are you going to be down there?" I asked her. I was ready for her to come home. If I was going to talk to anybody, Jordan included, I need her by my side.

"I'll be back in the morning, Luv. Get you some more rest. I told JJ to stay there with you. I will call Ma-Ma and tell her to keep Jordan away." She replied.

"Alright." I said getting back in the bed. I don't know how she knows these things, but I was tired as fuck. Not just physically, but mentally as well. I had decisions and moves to make. That shit wasn't going to get done today. I felt like I was recuperating from a night of drinking.

"I gotta go. Be good, baby." She said and hung up. I placed my phone on the charger and another incoming call came through. I thought Joel was calling me back when I answered.

"Please tell me that you changed your mind and that you are coming home baby."

"Jason." Mya said on the other end sounding surprised and shit. She never got conversation time with me. So, to hear that many words come out my mouth at once must have shocked the shit out of her. I took a deep sigh before I answered her.

"What do you want, Mya?" I said to her. I was already mad because I didn't screen her call.

"I was called on a job in Texas. I told them that I was finished with that type of work, but my clients were persistent about me doing this job. When I get back, I thought that we could sit down and talk about some things that have been going on with us." She replied. I didn't know if I was too subtle with her when she called last time. Clearly, she didn't get where I was coming from.

"I am not meeting up with you, Mya. Don't call my fucking phone again." I told her and was about to hang up when something she said stopped me.

"Jason, I'm pregnant." She said quietly.

"And." I replied. These hoes play entirely too much. I stayed strapped up before entering her pussy. I wasn't the only one she was fucking with. I knew that as well as her. Of course, I may have been the only nigga worth something. She fucked them stupid dancing ass niggas in the club. The ones that be practicing shit at home before they go out.

"What the fuck you mean 'And'? This is your baby, Jason. You need to man up and take care of your responsibilities." Mya said to me getting angry. I didn't understand why, though.

"Who the fuck you think you talking to?" I said as I sat up. I could feel myself ready to fly to Texas and snap this hoe neck. She got me fucked up for real.

"Look I just think-" she was trying to say before I interrupted her.

"I don't care what you think. Don't call my phone again. Make that my last time telling you this." I told her and hung up. I put my phone on vibrate and went to sleep like my baby asked.

SEVENTEEN
JORDAN

After leaving Joseph at the house, I headed to the other safe house on the countryside. I didn't know what I was going to tell my father when I reached the house. I didn't want to tell him the truth about what was going on. He would be pissed. My phone started ringing in the middle of me thinking of shit to tell him. I looked down and saw that it was Tristan. He was my connect that was helping me gather information about the first-born sons of the Stand. Jason took care of two of them. Ricky and Zeek took care of the other two. I had DJ and Roc left. Roc was going to be hard due to the power that his family had.

"What's up." I answered.

"Yo, we got a problem. Someone got into my system and tracked my recent activities." Tristan said loud and clear. I couldn't believe the shit that was coming out of his mouth, so I asked him to repeat himself. He said the same thing slower this time. I took a deep breath before responding.

"Nigga, I thought you were the best at what you do. How in thee fuck did that happen? Did you at least find out who it was?"

"Yeah," he said like I wanted to guess.

"Well, who muthafucker?" I yelled at his crazy ass.

"Yo, don't be yelling at me nigga. I found out who, but the shit is crazy. It was like he wanted me to find out who he was. He left an encrypted message with a Navy Cross behind it." Tristan kept talking, but at that point, my mind started racing. Jason found out my plans. He found out what my plans were and how Rick and Zeek were involved in it. I started hitting my steering wheel. This shit can't be happening right now. Jason was just like my father. He had disagreed with my plans and came to the house to take me out. Take us all out because of the operation I came up with. I had to find out what he knows before going to my father. A plan was forming in my head.

"Tristan, what did Jason find out?" I asked him. He pretty much knew it was Jason, being our cousin and all. My Aunt Glen stayed in the ATL with her two boys Tristan and Tank. Tank was like me. He ran shit down in ATL. I told him my ideas, and he agreed with them. He started pushing people off the Stand and was almost done. I just had to finish my part.

"Everything. He knows about Tank's operation as well." Tristan sighed his frustration. "Jason is going to kill us all, man. I'm feeling like Pac right nah, *I see death around the corner*." This asshole said serious as shit.

"Shut yo stupid ass up. Jason ain't coming out there. Just continue with everything. Me and JJ will take care of Jason. Tell Tank to push through, though. We might have to tell our parents what is going on earlier than we planned."

"Look, I don't want to be around Tee Joyce or my mom when y'all fools tell them about this shit. I will be on vacation nigga." Tristan told me and hung up the phone. My mother and Aunt Glenda were some bad women. Their twin brothers, Jerimiah and Jerry, were the head of their family. After my grandfather died, he told them to look out for their sisters. They both had plans, though. Even with Uncle Jerimiah being the oldest of the twins, Jerry wanted things his way. They argued and fought about everything. The people in their crew started dying, people started choosing sides, and their business started getting hit. My Tee Glen and my mother jumped in when Jerimiah killed their niece and Uncle Jerry's wife, Fallon.

Jerry killed Jerimiah's family while the sisters were talking to him at one of his businesses. Jerry showed up and pointed the gun to Jerimiah's head. Jerimiah did the same thing to Jerry. They were surrounded by their crew and everybody was at a loss for words. Before them fools could let out a shot, my mother and aunt took them out.

They didn't want to continue any of the businesses that the twins created, so they burned all that shit down. The sisters split up the contacts and connects, then rebuilt. My mother moved up north, and my aunt stayed down south to spread out the businesses of the Jones clan. My mother married my father which made the Jones of the North, the Stand. My father's family was already big out here. He let my mother's clan shine a bit before making her his. My mother was tired of all that shit anyway. She just wanted to be a mother and a wife of the family. She chose not to be involved.

I pulled up to the country house and got out. This house looked more southern than the rest. The wraparound porch gave it that southern look. It was white with green shutters. This house was wide and long, with five bedrooms and five baths. There were three acres of land behind the house and two in the front.

I walked in the door with Lilly pacing. She saw me and ran into my arms. "I'm ok, Lilly." I told her. She was still crying and trembling.

"I am not going nowhere else tonight. I just want you to rest for me. You are going to stress yourself out thinking about shit that you shouldn't be thinking of. Go upstairs and I will be right behind you after I talk to Pops." I told her while rubbing up and down her back. She looked at me and kissed me like I went to war. Fucking with Jason, you can say that.

"Ok, just hurry up. You know that I sleep better with you by my side." She said being very compliant and emotional. Tears started coming down her face. She wiped them away and turned to walk down the hallway to one of the bedrooms that were there.

My Pops and Mom were in the office of the house. I walked in and their eyes went to mine. I closed the door and took the seat in front of my dad. I thought Mom was going to leave, but she walked to the chair that my father was sitting in and stood next to him. "What is going on?" My father asked me.

"Jason found out what Rick was up to. He was family with the Mitchells. He got up with Curtis and planned a hit out on us. Jason been telling us about Rick being a snake for a while. I have been giving Rick access to a lot of shit because I thought he was loyal to the family. We all thought that. I put Rick too close to the fam." I told them. I was hoping that they didn't read into that shit too much. I really wasn't ready for the shit to come out yet. I wanted to set things up nicely for them to see that I had everything under control.

My father was looking at me like he didn't believe one damn word from my mouth. But, he does know how Jason get when the family let muthafuckers in to hurt us easily. My mother wasn't buying it at all. She shook her head and walked out of the office. The disappointment I saw on her face had me feeling some type of way. I knew I was lying to them. It burned my soul to do so.

"So, you mean to tell me, that Jason wanted to kill the family over Rick." My father asked calmly.

"We didn't trust his judgment. Wouldn't you feel some type of way about that, especially if Rick succeeded?" I asked him. I was feeling some type of way letting this nigga in too deep. He could have killed all of us when we were eating dinner at the house. My father was thinking about what I said and let out a sigh. I got up and walked to the bar in the office. I fixed me and my father a much-needed drink. I took my first drink straight down and made another one. I took my father his drink and placed it on the desk. He grabbed his drink and stared at me over his glass.

"Is there something else that you have to tell me?" He asked me before taking his drink.

"No," I said with a little of hesitation.

"Are you lying to me, Jordan?"

"Yes," I answered this time.

"When will you tell me the truth, Son."

"Soon, Pops. Real soon." I told him while drinking my second drink.

After having a few more drinks with Pops, I went upstairs to Lilly. She was still up waiting for me. I took a shower and crawled into the bed with her. I was mentally tired of all the shit that was going on around me. I woke up the next morning with my brothers on my mind. Joseph hasn't called or texted me yet. I grabbed my phone and saw that it was after ten. I called JJ and he didn't answer. I got up and put some grey sweats and a white t-shirt on. I grabbed my Retro 12 and keys and walked out the room. My mother was on the phone talking to someone and Lilly was picking at her breakfast. My dad must have been in his office. I was putting on my shoes when my mother spoke.

"JJ and Jason are ok. Joel said it will be best if we give Jason some time to calm down some more. She will call us when she returns from Louisiana." My mother said out loud. I know that she was still salty about what I said about Jason. I wanted to ease her mind, but she wasn't ready to hear what I had to say. She looked up at me and shook her head in disappointment. She slammed the plates on the table and walked out of the kitchen.

"What is going on Jordan?" Lilly asked quietly. She still wasn't eating her food. "Ma hasn't said anything all morning. She has been moving around like a zombie."

"Everything will be alright Lilly. I don't want you to worry about anything but keeping my baby girl healthy." I told her. I walked to stand behind her, grabbed a fork full of eggs, and fed it to her. I did that and talked to her until her food was gone. "Would you like to take a bath baby girl?"

"Yes. Only if you will take it with me." She said standing from the table. She reached out to kiss me, and my phone started ringing. I answered my phone without taking my eyes off Lilly.

"Yo," I answered, ready to get off the phone.

"Nigga, why didn't you tell me about Jason? You got me out here blind and shit." Tank hollered through the phone.

"Go to the bedroom; I'll be there in a minute." I said to Lilly and walked off without waiting for her to respond. I walked out the back door to continue the phone call with my cousin.

"Man, Jason ass is still at the house with JJ. He is not worried about y'all. I told your geeky ass brother that before I got off the phone with him. Did you finish on your end?" I asked him.

He sighed before answering me. "Yeah, I took out Lance last night. I'm having a meeting with the Stand Thursday at nine. If anyone disagrees with anything I say, I'm taking them out. I am tired of catering to these punk ass niggas. What about you?"

"Nah, Jason almost took us out last night. Joel had to step in and calm this nigga down. JJ is with him right now, but I know that I am going to have to confront this nigga about that shit. He had all of us on one." I replied to him.

"Oh, shit! That nigga lost it like that and you talking like shit ok. My mother would have fucked Jason up if he would have touched T Joyce. You know that she doesn't play behind her baby sister." This nigga said. I believed him too. My Auntie Glenda was crazy as fuck. "But, hold up, who is Joel?"

"She is a chick my mom met at the grocery store and invited to cook some Louisiana food for the family. Joel and Jason bumped heads every time that they were around each other. We saw that nigga getting soft behind her. He was about to murder that fool Rick when he suggested Joel for himself. And speaking of that nigga, Jason took him and his whole family out last night. He found out what that bitch ass nigga was up to." I told him looking back at the house.

"I don't want to get into all this shit right now, but I will finish my shit up before the week is out. Tell your brother to boost up his system. We can't have muthafuckers finding out shit beforehand." I told him and hung up the phone. I walked back into the house and my father was in the kitchen. He was drinking coffee and reading the paper.

"I need you to set up a meeting with the Stand at the end of the week. I want all of my sons at the table this time. We have a lot of shit to discuss. Make it happen." My father requested. Shit, no bath or pussy for me

EIGHTEEN

JASON

Mya kept calling and texting me about this baby. She lost her fucking mind. I ain't claiming shit that way. I could see if it was a possibility, but there wasn't one. I was sitting watching ESPN with JJ when Joel walked in. I got up and met my baby halfway. I grabbed her and hugged her tightly. I was kissing everywhere that was available to me.

"Nigga, you whack as fuck. Talking about pussy ain't the answer to everything. Here it is, Joel got you all strung out." Joseph said while changing the channel. I was about to reply but my baby beat me to it.

"This ain't no regular pussy, nigga." She said smiling up at me.

"No, it's not." I told her and picked her up to kiss her. She wrapped her legs around me and started pulling on my ears. That shit had me about to tell JJ to get the fuck out. I turned towards the bedroom when the front door opened. JJ and I went back into the main house after he woke up. He told me not trust no one in the crew because of the orders Jordan had put out. We were waiting for the person to appear in the doorway. I knew it was Jordan stepping through this bitch with Timberlands on. I put Joel down and took my shirt off.

Jordan appeared at the door with nothing but his dark grey

sweats and Timbs on. He had his dreads up in a ponytail. I had on my basketball shorts and Nike slides. I took my slides off and started grilling that nigga. I couldn't believe how much I hated him at that moment. I felt that cloud coming over me, but I refused to let it consume me that time. JJ told me that I owed it to Ma to let this nigga talk. He had three minutes.

He must have not known that those three minutes started when his stupid ass walked into the house. He was staring me down like he didn't owe me an explanation. JJ got up and walked between us to remind this nigga that I was giving him the chance to talk.

"Just tell us why, Jordan."

"Why what?" The nigga had the audacity to say.

"Fuck all this,' I said walking around JJ. I swung on that nigga, he blocked and grabbed me, to slam me on the floor. I wrapped my arm around that nigga's neck to lock us in that position, because if he slammed me, his ass was coming with me. He let me go and started hitting me with those body shots that wasn't hitting on nothing. I pushed that nigga back so that we could go head to head. He swung at me, I ducked, and it was a wrap for him after that. I hit him in the throat and then in the face. After that, shit became a blur for me. We were beating the shit out of each other. We had to be going at for at least fifteen minutes. Every swing he missed, I dodged it and hit that bitch under his arms. His punches started losing their weight and became weaker and slower. My next blow to his face laid his ass out. I got on top of him and locked his arms under my knees. I wrapped my hands around that bitch's throat and squeezed. I just wanted to feel the life leave that nigga's body.

I felt JJ on me, trying to pull me off him, but it was too late. I needed this shit like my last breath. The nigga was struggling underneath me. It wasn't going to be long now. JJ tried to put me in a sleeper to loosen up my hold on Jordan. He was talking about Ma and how disappointed she would be in me. But, this nigga was the reason why we are in this situation anyway. I felt his life slipping through my hands. His eyes got wide and my grin got wider.

"Jason, that is enough." Joel said, while standing in front of me.

I didn't listen to her this time and squeezed tighter. I felt hands on my arms and pain shot through my spine. I open my eyes and I was on the floor with Joseph. He was trying to calm me down, but I was stuck like a muthafucker. I twisted my head to the right and saw that Joel was standing over Jordan. She was telling him to breathe in the air slowly, so that he wouldn't choke. She was comforting this nigga in front of me. I threw JJ off of me and stood to walk back their way.

"Jason," she said in a chastising way.

I looked at her and she looked like she was ready to fuck me up. "Control yourself, baby. Please." She pleaded with me this time. This nigga didn't deserve a second chance. When she stopped me from killing that nigga the other night, I thought he knew to stay away from me. Jordan thinks that because he leads the family, that he is untouchable. I made him feel that way. Everybody knew that if you fucked with my family that I was coming for you and yours. Joel was handing this nigga another get out of jail free card.

"Jason, let him talk." JJ told me. That nigga was out of breath from wrestling me off Jordan. I stood there and waited for another three minutes or for this nigga to continue playing stupid. Joel looked at Jordan like 'start talking nigga' because that was her last time intervening.

Jordan sat up and looked like he was ready to attack me again. I smiled and prayed that he followed through. Joel walked towards me and stood in front of me with her back pressed against my stomach.

"Jordan, just talk," she warned this nigga.

Jordan stood up with his eyes still on mine. He shook his head and walked towards the bar. He tried to grab a glass, but his arms were feeling like jelly right now. JJ walked over to the bar and pushed him out of the way. He fixed that nigga a drink and sat it on the bar. Jordan looked down at the drink then at JJ.

"Bitch you better sip that shit through a straw." He said while fixing his own drink. I can feel myself losing my patience. I grabbed Joel's waist to move her when the nigga started speaking.

"The Stand should be ours. We brought everything to the table for the ungrateful bitches to use. Supplies, product, security, assassins, and any other things that them bitches need, we supply them. And we don't get shit from it. We are not their equals. We are better than them without that fucking table. We need to take over completely and start running this shit the way we feel fit, without the opinions of the others." He said pissing me off even more.

"That's your problem Jordan. You can't step in an organization that has been working for and with everybody for years, just because you disagree with how shit has been ran. If Pops felt that way in the beginning, he would not have offered territory and contacts to each family. We are not out here hurting, Jordan," JJ said trying to get this nigga back on that track he was talking about. Fuck that track. I wasn't worrying about getting this nigga back on. I was off the track my whole life, and his ass never thought to put or guide me the right way.

"You are a simple nigga, JJ. As long as your dick stay wet, nigga, you are always good. None of you see the bigger picture. I want us on top of everything. Niggas should come to us and only us if they want shit to happen. We don't have to conduct a meeting with the Stand." He said getting all fired up. "Them muthafuckers should fear us."

"Fuck you, nigga! That's not the only thing I think about. You out here being greedy and trying to take over something that's not all yours." JJ said to Jordan. He was tired of people thinking that he wasn't bringing nothing to the table. It was JJ's idea for the three clubs that was bringing in more money than the dealership.

"If you were a good leader, you would know that you cannot lead with fear." Joel said softly.

"What? Hey, I don't even know why you are here. This discussion ain't none of your fucking business. Go in the kitchen and bake something." This nigga faced her and yelled. I was about to attack that bitch when Joel held onto me tightly.

"Jordan, I need you to take the bass and the volume out of your tone. You know damn well if I wasn't here now and a few days ago, you and the family wouldn't be alive. So, don't come at me like that bruh. Every great leader knows that fear is not the way to run your empire. The men that you guys grew up around, were raised to not fear anything but God himself. Because all men on earth can bleed the same shit you do. Fear causes confusion. If a man like Jason, JJ, or even yourself fears someone that can take what you worked so hard to get, what would be the end results for that person?" She asked us all. I knew where she was going with this.

JJ seemed to understand it, too. "I'll off that nigga, fa real." JJ replied nodding his head to that true shit my baby was speaking.

"Right. You are supposed to lead with respect. Loyalty." She said letting my arms go.

"These niggas act the way they do right now because of the fear that your man put in these fools. Fear get these niggas to act right." Jordan said looking at me.

Joel shook her head and replied to this fool like he was slow as fuck. "And they will act out. Jason is not unstoppable. He can be beat just like the rest of them. If he is gone, the fear is eliminated, and it will leave the family open for anyone to try to take whatever that family has. Don't you see that?"

Jordan stared at her and looked away. He picked his drink up and took it with one gulp. "Dad want us all at the table for the meeting. Y'all need to be there."

"I'm not going to that shit." I said finally. I wasn't sitting around a table to discuss shit. "I'm done with this shit. Don't call me for nothing Jordan. We out." I said right before I grabbed Joel's hand and led her out the house. I left my shirt and Nike slides in the family room. I wasn't coming back to this house for a while. I can't keep coming around my family and not wanting to kill Jordan. I opened the passenger door of my car for Joel and walked around to the other side. Joseph was running out towards me.

"J, where are you going?" He asked me urgently. He knew that I was leaving with no chance of coming back. Jordan had the game fucked up fa real. I looked at my twin brother and hoped that he could understand where I was at this point with Jordan. He shook his head and looked down. "No J," he said disappointedly.

"Bye JJ." I told him and got into my car. I pulled off without a backwards glance. Joel grabbed my hand and rubbed it. She didn't say anything but her being here speaks volume. JJ was right from the beginning, I needed a break. I needed to get away from all this shit that was surrounding me. If I didn't, the darkness was going to consume me. I started thinking about all of the things that could have driven me to that point. If I would have killed my family, I knew that I would have lost it then. Not noticing that my feet was pushing down on the gas pedal, we were doing seventy-five on the main road.

Joel squeezed my hand a little to get my attention. She didn't panic or yell like the average chick would. "Pull over, Jason." She said softly. I swerved over onto the side of the road. I was about to lose it fa real. Joel snatched off her seatbelt, reached over, and pulled my dick out of my basketball shorts. She took my man down her throat with no problems. I pulled her up by her hair to push my seat further back. She crawled over to me and got onto her knees. She dragged my shorts all way down to my ankles. She started stroking me with her eyes on me. I don't know what her hands were made of, but the shit had me leaning back and moaning like a bitch in heat.

She licked and sucked the underside of my dick. That had to be the most sensitive part of my shit. My baby looked up at me and eased me in her mouth until her nose hit my pelvic bone. That shit alone had me spilling my shit down her throat. I didn't care that it only took me a couple of minutes to bust. Any woman that can pull a nut out of a nigga that quick without trying was a beast. But, I hope she knew that this shit wasn't over. My shit was still standing at attention and that dark cloud was still over my head. She looked up at me and smiled. "You taste good, daddy. Let's get home so we can finish this, shall we."

"Nah, we are about to finish this right now." I told her as I pulled her on top of me. I reached under her dress and ripped her thong off. I pushed up into her and her pussy latched onto my dick like a baby would a nipple for breast milk. She rotated her hips slowly while grabbing my ears tightly.

"It's ok baby. I am here and I'm not going anywhere." She told me out of the blue.

I knew she wasn't going anywhere; if she tried I would hunt her down and lock her ass up. She was whispering some more shit in my ear that had darkness melting away. You could hear the wetness of her pussy over the traffic that was passing us by. I grabbed her ass and tried to speed up her winding, but she didn't allow me to. She wanted us to go at her pace even though this moment was for me. I pulled her dress down to suck on her titties. I bit down on her nipple and then soothed it with my tongue. She got wilder with each bite. After some long stroking and slow grinding, we both came with some loud groans. I pulled her from my neck and stared. She was biting on her bottom lip and smirking at me at the same time.

"Are you good, baby?" She asked while caressing my face.

"Yeah, I'm good." I said giving her a kiss on those sexy ass lips.

"Good, because now we can go and see Ma-Ma and Pops before we leave for our vacation." She said as she adjusts her dress. This woman amazed me. I didn't tell her anything about a vacation. But, just like JJ, she read my mind and knew what I needed. What I didn't want to do right now, is to see my parents. I didn't want to see the disappointment on their faces. No matter how old you get, you always want to make your parents proud of you.

"I'm not ready, El." I told her pulling back on the road, driving the speed limit this time.

"I promise Ma-Ma that I was going to bring you over to see her before we leave." She said as she was texting on her phone.

I turned my head to see if she was one of the X-Men. Professor X's daughter or some other fucking mutant. "Where are we going? And, how did you know that I wanted to leave?" I asked her.

"I know after the way you looked at Jordan that it won't be long before you act out the thoughts in your head. I thought that maybe we can go somewhere for a while to clear your head. Get you away from all this negativity and relax a little. Ma-Ma agrees with me. Your parents are at the country house waiting on us to pass by." She told me still texting on her phone.

"Who are you texting on the phone?" I asked her while making a u-turn and driving towards the country house.

"My BFF Tyja. I am letting her know that I am coming home. She house-sits for me when I go out of town on business or just because. You will meet her and a couple more of my friends when we get there." She replied.

"Who said I was going to New Orleans?" I asked her. I would have gone wherever she wanted to go. I just wanted her to keep talking to me. Joel was easy to talk to. Her voice and accent turned me on. The way she called me baby and asked me questions without giving me time to answer and ask another one. She would say some shit like "that shit was good, fa real, huh." The shit didn't make any sense to me but that sexy drawl in all her words had my dick rising again.

"Down boy." She told me looking down at my basketball shorts, laughing and shaking her head.

I pulled up to the house twenty minutes later. My baby jumped out the car and waited for me to get out. I got out and walked around to the back of my car. I popped the trunk and pulled out some more Nike slides and a fresh shirt. I closed the trunk and took a deep breath with my eyes closed. When I opened my eyes, Joel was staring up at me.

"I'm here and I am not going anywhere." She repeated to me reaching for my hand. I grabbed it and led her to the house. Before we could make it to the front door, it opened with my mom smiling at me. I smiled back and that gave her the go to jump into my arms.

"My baby boy. I am so happy to see you." She said holding onto me tightly. I held her and wanted to apologize for what I had done. The apology wasn't for what I was going to do, but for why I had to do it. To hear that her son was just like her twin brothers, was going to have my mother pissed off. The only thing that was different about Jordan was that he wanted everybody in the Davis and Jones crew to shine. He never put himself above us, but above the others in the Stand.

"Come in, son; we have a lot to discuss." She said pulling me in.

I grabbed Joel's hand and pulled her in with me. I wasn't going to be able to tell her the shit that was going on. Unlike my brothers, I tell my mother everything. But, this was going to be something that I was going to have to fabricate a little. I knew she had spoken to Jordan already and saw through whatever bullshit story he told her. That's why she felt that we had a lot to discuss. We walked into the kitchen where Pops and Lilly were sitting. Lilly was staring at me. I gave her a reassuring look and went to give her a hug.

"Congratulation," I told her. She smiled up at me and let out a deep breath. I know that she was still scared and confused about what happened the other night. "Thank you, big brother. Your niece or nephew needs you and their father to be on good terms." She said to me. I couldn't promise her that, so I didn't respond. My pops got up and stared at me. That nigga Jordan looked so much like Pops. I felt Joel grab and squeeze my hand to keep me focused I looked down at her and nodded.

"Son," Pops asked.

"Yeah Pops," I replied to him. He walked over to me and pulled me in a hug like Ma did. He pulled back and told me that he loved me. "I love you, too, Pops. But y'all gotta do something about Jordan before he destroys an empire that wasn't built on his blood, sweat, and tears." I told my father in a whisper. Lilly and my mom were gathered around Joel. I didn't want to upset Lilly in her condition.

My Pops nodded his head. "I know, son, that is why I want all of you guys at the meeting on Friday. Even though what Jordan did was fucked up, we can't show them that we are divided. After the meeting, we will talk about some new roles for you and JJ." He was saying, but I wasn't trying to hear this shit. I wanted to get the fuck out of here for a while. I didn't know how long I was going to be. I just know that this business was toxic, and I needed to pull back and evaluate some shit.

"Nah, Pops. I won't be making the meeting. I will be going on a vacation with Joel." I told him. I was ready for him to argue when he smiled tiredly. He pulled me into another hug and kissed me on my cheek.

"Wow, it took a woman to get you to do what me and your mother been begging you to do. You must really like her." My Pops said. His ass was just like Mom. He was fishing for things that I wasn't ready to admit yet. I looked him in the eyes and told him how sorry I was. "I never meant to disrespect you or Ma like that. Jordan is fucking shit up Pops. I know that you are ready to retire from this business, but I don't think Jordan was ready to lead Pops." He shook his head and walked near the window. I followed behind him to get away from the women. He took a deep breath before he started speaking.

"Do you remember when we went to that hotel for a meeting with Francis. You and JJ didn't want to sit in the meeting with me and Jordan, so I asked you guys to chill out until we were done. When we were finished with the meeting, Jordan and you wanted to go swimming. You guys were in the pool while JJ was sitting on the side. That was the first time I have ever seen him so afraid. I saw how badly JJ wanted to be in there with his brothers. So, I pushed him in with y'all." My father laughed as he reminisced on some shit I didn't find funny.

"Joseph was screaming for help, like we were going to let him drown. When he saw how we came to his rescue the first time, he jumped in the second time on his own. As a parent, it is my job to catch my children when they fall and push their fears away when it stops them from achieving anything. Jordan is falling, Jason. What type of father would I be if I sat and watched that happen. He wasn't ready, true. But, he has me and the rest of his brothers to back him. Just like Joseph did. Just like you will." My father told me while staring at me. I didn't want to hear this shit right now. I just wanted to get away and be different. My Pops must have recognized that because he grabbed me by shoulders.

"Go on son. Have a great time and come back with a fresh mind." He said to me.

"I am coming with y'all. I want to see the city of New Orleans just like the next one. Lilly, pack your shit too. You are coming with us as well. Fucking around with Jordan, you will be eating Hot Pockets and shit." My mother said walking towards her bedroom. Lilly walked after her without disagreeing with her. Joel and my father were talking, and I was wondering what was going on. I am not going on vacation with three women. I interrupted Pops and Joel's conversation to tell them that.

"Hey Pops, you are going to have to cancel your meeting. I am not going nowhere with all these women." Pops and Joel laughed as my mother came in with her suitcases walking towards the front door. Lilly was behind her giggling at my annoyance. Joel kissed Pops and followed behind the women.

Pops walked me to the door as the women walked out. "Come back when you are ready son and watch your Mom. Two of those suitcases are empty. She is preparing to buy a lot of shit." He laughed. My mom walked back towards us to kiss my dad bye. Lilly also came over to hug and kiss Pops He squatted to speak to his grandchild. "Be good for your mother, boy, or I will get you when you come out." We watched Dad continue with his conversation when Jo pulled up with JJ. I dapped my Pops up and walked to my dad's Escalade without acknowledging any of them niggas.

Jordan looked pissed that Lilly was leaving without talking to him. Mom jumped in his ass and told him to get the fuck on. Yeah, she was big mad at this nigga. Lilly kissed Jordan and jumped into the SUV. I pulled off with the women talking about women shit and that alone had me wishing that I would have had the conversation with them over the phone.

NINETEEN

JORDAN

That nigga had my body hurting. I forgot how hard his ass can hit. When he walked out the house with Joel, I collapsed in the chair at the bar. I leaned back and coughed up blood. I couldn't blame him for feeling the way he did. What bothered me the most is the shit that came out of Joel's mouth. The shit she was spitting was true; I just didn't want to hear it. JJ walked back in the house like he lost his best friend. I knew he was about to go in on me as well. I sat up straighter and prepared myself for his lecture.

"Why you lied to me, Jordan? We are supposed to be doing this shit together and you got me out here looking all kinds of stupid. You let Rick and Zeek into your plans nigga and they ain't even blood. You had me thinking I was bugging when I told you about using Jason for them kills. All along you had your own agenda. Let me know something right now, Jo, or I am out, just like Jason." He told me angrily. I knew that JJ was hurt for what Jason told him. Now that it was out, I was happy that I didn't have to go into details with him about my plans.

"Look JJ, I didn't want to get you involved. I knew that your views lined up the same way as Pops. You were going to try and talk me out it. And after all that would have failed; you would have created an intervention group. I just didn't have time for all that JJ. I saw the opportunity and I moved. I wanted my brothers on it with me badly, bruh." I told JJ the truth.

"Jo, I can see if you were making a change that will help us all in the long run, but you're not. You are making long-term enemies that our children would have to face when they get older. That's why Pops did what he did. He didn't want us battling his wars. He doesn't want us to create one either. How can you not see that?" JJ said, trying to get me to understand where he was coming from. At this point, it was too late to go back on anything that I have done. In a little bit, Pops was going to receive a phone call from his friend saying that DJ was eliminated. I only had Roc left.

"I killed DJ last night. Roc is next. His parents have a dinner party on Saturday. I was trying to get rid of him before then. Hopefully, with all of the killings, they will have to push the meeting back so that I can get to Roc. If not, I will have to get him at his club downtown. Whether you in or out JJ, this is going to happen. It is too late for me to turn back now." I told him. He was quiet for a minute. He was still trying to find a way to redo all the shit that I have done. In order to make things right, they will have to take me or a member of my family out. JJ walked over to me. He held his hand out to me to help me out of the chair. "Let's go see Pops, man. We gotta let him and Ma know that Jason will be leaving. Ma is going to kick your ass fa sure this time."

"Shit man, let's stop and get me some headgear." I told JJ as we walked out of our family home.

We drove to the country house in pure silence. JJ was still thinking of ways to end this shit, whereas I was thinking ways to end them all. When the members of the Stand find out it was me that put this shit together, I want it to be too late for retaliation. My phone began to beep. It was a text coming through. I opened it up and found pictures of Curtis and his girl dead with others around them. The shit was sick. Gage really put in work on these fools. We were pulling up when I saw everybody outside with luggage and shit. Lilly was putting her bags in the back of my Pops' Escalade. I jumped out the car and Lilly told me that she was going on vacation with my family.

"I don't think that it is a good idea to leave at this moment." Jason passed me by without a glance. My mother told me to get the fuck out of the way and that Lilly was going no matter what. I kissed her and held her tightly. "I love you and you feed my baby." I told her. I know with Jason being mad at me, he still wouldn't let anything happen to Lilly. She was like the little sister he didn't have. They got into the SUV and pulled out. I walked into the house after my brother and father. We walked into the office and took a seat. Before we could say anything to each other, my father phone went off. JJ looked at me and shook his head.

My father picked the phone up and answered, "Yeah." He listened to the caller on the other end. His facial features changed with every word that was said. "I'm sorry to hear that Derrick. Let me know what I can do." My father said before hanging up the phone.

He looked at me with fire in his eyes. "They canceled the meeting with the Stand. DJ was killed in his home last night. They said it was somebody he knew. There were no signs of forced entry or struggle." He stood and continued talking. "Derrick said that DJ had to know the dude, because he doesn't let just anyone into his private home." My father was now standing over me. "You need to tell me what I need to know ASAP." He demanded.

TWENTY

When we got to New Orleans, we were hit with that special heat. I was pretty much used to it, but my mother and Lilly looked like fishes out of the water. We stopped at the first store to get a pop. Joel laughed at my request.

"What the hell are you laughing at?" I asked her.

"I forgot how y'all talked up there. Let me get a pop." She said making fun of my accent.

We went back and forward about that shit until we reached her home in a suburban area in the east of New Orleans. We walked in and there was a big chandelier hanging in the foyer. She had the same picture of the Quarters hanging up on the wall but this one was painted. She also had pictures of Mardi Gras floats and Indians. You can tell how much she loves her city.

"Okay you guys, let's go upstairs to y'all rooms." Joel said while directing us to the stairs. "Each suite has its own master bathroom with a king size bed and a 70-inch 4k flat screen. Ma-Ma, you can watch all your TV shows as loud as you want because the walls are also soundproof." She said winking at my Mom. My mother started smiling all wide and shit. She looked at Lilly and they both were making faces at me. They were acting like some high school girls. Joel walked them to their rooms and told them to relax. "In a few, we are going to the grocery store to make some groceries."

Lilly and my mom came out of their room. The statement she just made didn't make any sense, but she was talking about me asking for a pop. "How do you make groceries, Joel." I asked the question that was all over Lilly's and Mom's faces. She turned around and smirked up at me. I knew her explanation was going to be stupid and was only going to make sense to her. She put her hand on her hip and explained.

"You get a basket..."

"A shopping cart," I interrupted her.

She ignored me and continued what she was saying. "You walk around the grocery store with it. You put stuff in the "basket" to make groceries because you are getting more than one item. If we were going to the store to get one or two things without the basket, then you are getting a couple of things from the store." She said like that shit was final. The women behind me started laughing because they knew that I wasn't going to let this go.

"Why can't you gather the groceries?" I asked her. She looked at me and her smirk became a full-blown smile.

"The same way you can't get a cold drink instead of a pop." She told me and walked towards the other bedroom.

I looked back at the women and they were still laughing. I shook my head and continued to follow Joel. She walked us into her bedroom and it was something to see. The colors were purple and gold. The room looked like royalty. There was a sitting area in the middle of the floor. Her king size bed was pushed to the back wall with two-night stands on each side. Golden lamps were sitting on the top of them. I walked in and looked to the left. A double vanity mirror with his and hers sink was outside the master bathroom. She also had pendant lights in that area. To the right, there were two balcony doors with another painting in between.

This one was hard to decipher. Before I could ask about it, she came out of some double doors near the bathroom.

"Hey, you can put your things in here on the right side." She said to me. I walked in there and the right side was completely empty. I placed my things there and came back out. She was standing by her balcony doors when I walked behind her and hugged her from behind.

"Thank you for this." I told her in a whisper.

She turned around and stared at me. "You are so welcome." She replied and kissed me softly. "Let's go to the store." She said excitedly.

I have never seen anyone so happy to go the grocery store. It was like her shopping mall. We all jumped in the car, with her driving us to a store called Rouses. We were in this grocery store for almost thirty minutes. Lilly and Mom were enjoying themselves. I walked behind the trio like a secret service agent. Every once in a while, Joel would look back and give me that sweet smile. I couldn't wait to get her back to that house and test out those soundproof walls. They turned down the last aisle and bumped into a woman and some of her friends.

"I'm sorry, baby. I didn't see you." Joel said to the woman.

"I am not your baby. Watch where you are going next time." The woman said to my girl.

I knew that fucking voice and I know that this bitch wasn't that bold to follow me here. I walked up to the woman and saw Mya and three other women with her.

"Hey J, what are you doing down here?" She asked me while rubbing on her belly. I stared at her and the bitch started smiling. She looked at my mom and spoke to her. "You must be Ms. Joyce, how are you? Jason told me so much about you. I am Mya. I was hoping that we get together before the baby was born."

My mother glared at me and Mya. This bitch got me fucked up. I don't know how she found out my mother's name. I would never give her that type of information about myself. I gotta contact Dex and tell him to look this hoe up, but in the meantime, I was going to choke this hoe out. I took a step forward and Joel jumped in front of me. I thought she was about to go off on me, but she didn't. She gave me a supportive smile and turned back towards the women.

"Lilly, let's get the rest of the items and get in the checkout line. I know you are tired from all this walking." She said to Lilly. Lilly shook her head in disagreement.

"Nope, I'm fine right here." Lilly said mugging Mya and her girls. Joel grabbed her arm and pushed her slightly to get her to start walking.

"Yeah, you do that while me and my man discuss our baby with my mother-in-law. I'm sure you can cook for the baby shower." Mya said to Joel. I was texting Dex Mya's information. There was no way for her to know about Joel and her relationship with the family. Joel stopped and turned towards us. I recognized that face too well. Joel was about to speak her mind and for the first time, I won't be on the other end of her assault.

"Don't get it twisted boo. I am walking off because it would be stupid to argue facts with you. I know who he belongs to, your mother-in-law knows too. And the baby you're carrying isn't my business, until he tells me different. Now, if you will excuse me, I have dinner to prepare for my family." Joel walked over to me and pulled me down by my ears to meet her in a sexy ass kiss. "I'll be in the checkout line when you're done with your situation." She said to me and walked off with Lilly. You can hear Lilly's loud ass in the next aisle laughing.

My mother was smiling but still glaring at Mya. She turned to me and asked me a question. "Son, do you have something to tell me?"

I looked down at my mother and answered her with no hesitation. "No, nothing at all."

My mother nodded and turned to walk away. "Well, let's go then. We don't want to keep both of my daughters-in-law waiting." I followed behind her without addressing Mya and her bullshit. I see that she was going to make me put my hands on her. I approached

Lilly and Joel with my mother in the line. They were talking as if that shit never happened. I loaded the car up and jumped on the passenger side. Joel was driving and listening to the radio. I stared at my baby girl, wondering where she came from. The display at the grocery store should have been chaotic.

"Why are you staring at me like that?" Joel asked.

"You surprise me. You handle that situation very...."

"Maturely" she interrupted. I nodded my head. She shook hers and continued talking. "What did you expect? A ghetto display with a trifling ass baby mama, who thinks that getting pregnant would keep a man. No, J, I don't stress myself out over shit I can't control and things that happened before me."

"How do you know that it happened before you?" I asked out of curiosity alone. She stopped at the stop light and looked at me.

"Because, you know better." She told me with her eyes blazing. She rolled her eyes and dared me to say anything else. My mother was absolutely right about Joel. She didn't give a fuck about who I was or what I have done in the past. She challenged and encouraged me at the same time. That fucking mouth was lethal. I could think of many ways to...

"Oh hell, he is giving her that look. The look Jordan gives me when he wants to do some really naughty things to me." Lilly said interrupting my thoughts. My mother leaned forward and smirked.

"Yep, that's the look. The infamous Davis men look. All I ask of you son, is to let me get out of the car first. I don't need to be seeing that shit." Lilly laughed and agreed with my mom.

"Me too. Oh, and I got to get my ice cream." Joel pulled into her driveway with the same heat in her eyes as mine.

Without taking my eyes off hers, I answered my mom and Lilly, "You have sixty seconds."

TWENTY-ONE
JORDAN

It's been a couple of days since I told my father what was going on. Disappointment wasn't the word to describe how he felt. He walked off from me. Because if he didn't, he was going to shoot me. But, JJ didn't let me slide. When Pops left the room, JJ punched the shit out of me. We all took it hard if any of our parents were hurting or disappointed in any of us. My mother caught JJ and one of his girls cutting school in our house. The girl was giving JJ head. My mother told JJ to bring the girl home and come back to the house. JJ didn't come back until midnight.

My mother was waiting for him with Matilda. They started arguing and JJ stood over Mom like he was going to do something. Jason came out of nowhere and tagged that boy in his jaw. I pulled my mother back and let Jason put that work on JJ. I held Mom back from interfering. Jason and JJ were up in their breaking shit up. When they were done, JJ needed to go to the hospital for a broken arm, nose, and needed seventeen stitches. When Pops came home from his business trip, he whipped JJ ass again.

I was with Brian and Jeff. We have been looking for Roc's ass for a week. His parents canceled the party and now none of them could be found. On the other hand, our shipments and the club downtown had been taking major hits. The club was shot up three times this week. Someone robbed each shipment that came in from the east and west side of Philly. Two of the judges that we were dealing with were dead, along with their families. This shit was crazy. We were headed to the center for a meeting. I know that the streets been talking. I had my crew out there squeezing information from the people in all territories. JJ and Pops were trying to reach out to the other contacts but haven't been getting any information from them. Something wasn't right about this.

I pulled up at the center and jumped out my Ford 450. I walked into the center with my crew following me. When I got to the front, I knew that the news that I was going to get was fucked up by the way these niggas was looking at me. The young soldier Victor didn't wait for me to ask a question. He started talking as soon as he saw my face.

"Yo Boss, the Stand has been having meetings and shit without the Davis crew. My cousin who work for Roc told me to get the fuck away from the crew because they were taking the Davis crew down. That's why the club been getting shot in and the shipments have been short. They been hitting our shit Boss."

I showed them no emotion. No fear. This was the war that JJ was talking about. I'm not going to front and act like I didn't want it. I knew that it was going to be hard to take down Roc and his crew. I never expected them to hold a meeting about it though. It was all good. The contacts that they did take was not a fraction of what we had. How the saying goes? Never tell your right hand what your left hand was doing. I still had my cousin and the rest of his crew down south ready for this war. I stood up and was ready to address the bullshit when a car came through our warehouse. Everyone jumped out of the way and started shooting at the car.

"Shoot out the tires," someone yelled. Brian popped two of the tires and the car came up to a slow stop. I approached the car with my gun drawn. There were two bodies in the car with a note stabbed into the chest of the driver. The body was burned and beaten so badly, their face was unrecognizable. Brian reached into the car and grabbed the note. He passed it to me without saying anything. I grabbed and read it. *"Coming for your legs."*

"Everybody get to my parents' house. NOW!"

Jordan and Mya were calling my phone back to back. I don't know if them niggas was sitting next to each other and taking turns calling me or what. But, the shit was aggravating. Joel's best friend Tyja came by and met the family. You can see the wheels turning in my mother's head. She was trying to find a way to get Tyja up to Philly to meet Joseph. I looked at Joel and she shook her head knowing what Ma was trying to do. She was taking pictures and snapping selfies of her and Tyja. She sent them to JJ and told him, look how good I look with my other daughter-in-law. JJ's stupid ass replied, *bring her home then.*

When Joel introduced me to Tyja, I reached my hand out to hers and she pulled me into a hug.

"We hug family down here," she told me. She pulled back and smiled up at me. "Thank you, for putting that smile on my girl face." She told me and then kissed me on my cheek. She just didn't know that I was the one doing all the smiling now. My mother and Lilly went back to Philly yesterday after spending a week down here. They both loved the city, but the heat wasn't something that they could deal with. My mom left with all types of Louisiana seasonings. I have been having a great time down here in New Orleans. The people were friendly and the food that I already fell in love with, had me feeling good. We were now on our way to my friend, Sincere's club.

My baby was dressed in some dark True Religion jeans, a red shirt with her back out and red stilettos. I had on some black True Religion jeans and a black V-neck. I also wore my black and red Jordan's with a black fitted hat. I was driving her 2017 black Range Rover to Magic Mic. She called her friend Tyja to tag alone. Tyja was meeting us at the club. She was at the house with me and Joel baking all types of sweets. She left to get ready at her house. I pulled up to the VIP valet service. The dude opened the door to help Joel out and I almost fucked him up. He was looking at her drooling and shit. This is why I hate going to clubs. These muthafuckers didn't respect shit. I got to him and Joel once again interfered.

"Let it go baby. We good." She said while grabbing my hand and walking me into the crowded club. We turned left to walk up the stairs to the VIP section. There were three love seats and a bar. We were able to look over the balcony into the crowd. The shit was tight. There was a woman with her back turned from us. "Damn Tyja, you here already. I thought I was going to be calling your ass in the next hour." Joel said to her best friend. She turned around and smiled at Joel. Mom hit that shit on the nail with Tyja. She was that slim chocolate that JJ would fall in love with. Of course, he fucks them all, but this would be the chick I called sister-in-law. I guarantee that.

"Gurl, you think that I would be late going out with my sis and my new brother. Nah, bitch, I was here before the crowd." Joel walked to her and gave her a hug like they hadn't seen each other earlier. "I missed you sis," Joel said. I reached out my hand for a handshake and she pulled me into a hug.

"I thought I explained this to you already nigga. We hug family down here." She told me and pulled back. She thanked me again and I looked at her confusedly. Why would she be thanking me like this? Joel must have been dealing with some fuck boys before me. She shook her head and started talking to Joel.

"It's good to finally see you out with the norms." A voice said behind me. I turned and Sincere was smirking at me. He was my nigga in my Seal crew. He was the one that didn't have a filter or brakes on his words. His ass was deadly with any gun that he had in his hand. I walked up to him and reached out to shake his hand. "Nigga I know you heard Lil Mama back there; we hug family down here." He said pulling me into a brotherly hug. I laughed, joked, and reminisced about our days as a Seal. We were there for at least an hour and a half drinking and talking. Joel stood up with Tyja and excused herself to the restroom. When the ladies were downstairs, Sincere leaned in to talk some serious shit.

"Man, did you hear about Matthews." I shook my head no.

"I didn't keep in contact with none of them boys, but you and Dex. Why, what happened?"

"Dude went crazy, man. We all felt how deep we were falling. I mean, we were turning into straight savages. We all were fucked up when we went in, but Matthews was certifiably fucked up. He took out the whole team and went AWOL after that." He told me. He was right though. We were all falling at a point of no return. That was why I got out. The reason that a few of us got out. I couldn't tell the difference between reality and my nightmares.

"Did they find out anything? Why he did it?" I asked him.

"Nope, he disappeared. No one has seen or heard from him since." Sincere replied. I was happy that he was out. He had a little sister to look after. We talked a little more when the man announced the next singer. I stood and walked to the balcony with Sincere. He was smiling like he knew what was going on. Joel walked on stage and smiled up at me. Tyja was standing on the side of the stage supporting her friend. Joel walked to the mic and started singing.

Through drought and famine, natural disasters
My baby has been around for me
Kingdoms have fallen, angels be calling
None of that could ever make me leave

I LISTENED to Joel sing about how she felt about me. I knew what she was really telling me and it took everything in me to let her finish the song. I was about to snatch her off the stage and find the nearest wall. My baby sounded so beautiful. Her deep, soulful voice was heard through the surround sound speakers. She sung the song, substituting some of the words. After she was done, she took a bow and walked off the stage. I dapped Sincere up and walked down the stairs to meet her halfway. When I reached her, I grabbed her arm and walked out of the club.

"I'll see you guys later." Tyja yelled behind us. I guess Sincere was reading my mind and mood because the Range Rover was parked in front. I opened the door and placed her in. I ran over to the driver side, hopped in, and pulled off with one destination in mind. We made it to her house in less than thirty minutes. I pulled into the garage and got out. Joel was already walking to the door, when I came up behind her. I grabbed her and turned her towards me.

"Tell me," I told her. She looked into my eyes and wrapped her arms around my neck.

"I love you, Jason," she replied so sweetly. Our sex was slow and passionate that time. I couldn't keep my eyes or my hands off of her. For the first time ever, I didn't want to cause pain during sex. I wanted her to feel good. And she did. After our last orgasm, we fell asleep.

I woke up out of a deep sleep three hours later from a nightmare. It was of the faces of the people I have killed. They were surrounding me and Joel. Their eyes were on her. They tried to attack her, and I turned feral. I was killing them off, but they kept coming. They all jumped on me and made me watch as they tore her apart. Joel woke up and reached for me. I slapped her hand away and tried to get up. But she crawled on top of me and tried to calm me down.

"It's ok, Jason."

"Get the fuck off of me, Joel." I told her tired and angrily.

"No, Jason. I am here and I'm not going anywhere. I can deal with the nightmares and all the ugliness that surrounds you. I love you for the man that you are, and the man that you are trying to become. You deserve happiness. You deserve to be loved, Jason. Just let it happen and stop fighting it." She told me softly.

"I don't deserve shit. You don't know what I have done, how many people I have killed just to satisfy some sick need. You don't know shit." I yelled at her and tried to throw her off me. She latched onto my arms and made me listen to her.

"Let it go, Jason. Baby, you don't have to be that man anymore. You can live a better life than that. Just let me show you." She told me. I wanted what she was offering, but didn't think a man like me could reach those types of heights. I wanted to let the shit go and live in peace with Joel.

"I killed so many." I whispered. I closed my eyes and again saw the faces of my victims. The darkness started creeping back in.

"Keep your eyes open, Jason. Stay here with me. Feel me, baby. This is real." She said to me while massaging my dick. "Focus on me, baby. The here and the now. Listen to my voice."

Joel kept talking me off the ledge. I opened my eyes to this beautiful woman. She leaned in and kissed me softly while placing my dick inside her. "Stay with me," she kept repeating over and over. I pulled her down to take her lips in mine. "I love you, Jason." She repeated with her forehead against mine. She rocked back and forth until we both reached our orgasm. I pulled her back from me and stared into her eyes. I wanted to tell her how I felt, but the words weren't ready to come out.

"Whenever you're ready." She said with understanding. She kissed me and rested her head on my chest. "You will have to let that shit go with Jordan, Jason. You know that your mother and father will be upset if anything happens to any of you. You just have to reevaluate some of your techniques or the laws that you guys created. I'm pretty sure that once the other members in the Stand finds out what Jordan has been up to, shit is going to go left really quick. Don't let the others see how divided the family is. Keep that shit in-house. Be there for your family, babe. Not the way they want you to be, but a way that will keep you out the darkness." Joel said to me.

Baby girl was trying to find a way to pull me and my brother back together. My mom mentioned it twice before she left. JJ called and told me to speak with him as well. "I'll think about it El." I told her with my hands rubbing up and down her back.

"Don't think about it Jason. Don't spend so much time on something that you can't control baby. You will lose your mind doing that. If beating his ass again will help you to forgive him, do that. Just let it go, baby." She replied and kissed me on my chest. A few minutes later, my baby fell asleep. I was thinking about the things she was saying. I really needed to come up with some changes for the Davis organization.

WE RETURNED to Philly a week after that night with Tyja. She told Joel that, if there were specimens like me up north, she was coming to get one. Joel let her know that I had a single brother and Tyja damn near jumped in the car without luggage. These women were entertaining. I haven't laughed this hard ever in life. I was at my home with the girls cooking and joking in the kitchen. Joel wanted to take Tyja to the mall to grab a few things for her. I gave her my Black card and told her to use it. Of course, she argued with me about it, but Tyja took the card and dragged Joel out the house.

I called Mom and she told me that everybody was acting strangely. I promised her that I would pass by to check things out. After the talk that me and Joel had, I felt that difference in myself. Every burden that I was holding, was being left behind with the guilt and all the other bullshit. I started getting dressed when my phone started ringing. I picked it up and saw that it was Mya. This bitch really didn't get it. Why is it when you try to be the better person, people start fucking with you? Mya was one of those people. That stunt she pulled down in New Orleans earned her another conversation with me.

"Hello," I answered, letting my voice drop and the coldness through.

"J-Jason. We need to talk about the baby." She replied unsure of herself.

"It's funny how you take me to play with. I already told yo simple ass what it was. But, you insist that the baby is mine. So, I am going to give you two options. Option A: you leave me the fuck alone. Nice and simple right," I waited for her to answer me back. She already knew that I have reached my limit with this foolishness.

"Right!" I yelled at her.

"Right," she said now terrified of the way things were about to go.

"Or you can take Option B: I come around and spend some time with you during the pregnancy. Take a test when the child is born. If she or he is not mine, I get to cut both of y'all open and feed y'all to your parents for dinner." I told her letting some of that darkness through. It wasn't completely gone out of my system. It was good to have some type of control over it. I heard her breathing heavily on the phone like she was on the verge of crying.

"I don't know why you are doing this to me." She told me. "I was there for you when you needed me to be and now you talk to me like I don't matter."

"You don't. Now choose A or B."

"Fuck you, Jason." She yelled and hung up the phone. She made the right choice. I really didn't feel like killing any more babies. That shit took a piece of your soul every time. I shook my head to keep myself from thinking of it too much. My baby was teaching me things to help me be normal. I was thinking of having a family of my own. Mom would be happy to hear that. I just hoped that my kids took after their mother.

TWENTY-THREE

JORDAN

"Bruh, Tank and his crew said that they will be here in a few hours. Let's wait with the rest of the plans. I'm pretty sure them niggas got some ideas that can finish off the Stand." JJ said to me.

We were at this shit for days when we found out what them hoe ass niggas were doing. I couldn't wait to wrap my hands around Roc's neck. This bitch thought he was king up here. He told the people that were working for my family, that we were finished and under the Browns. I went to his house and his parents' crib. I wasn't with this hiding shit. I was ready to confront this nigga head on.

JJ told me to play it smart and think of other ways to hit this fool. They were about their money just like us. We were planning on hitting all the Brown's businesses at the same time. Joseph was going after their accountant for all of their banking information with Tristian. After we were done with that, they will have no choice but to come out of hiding. Scary ass niggas.

"Aight. As soon as they touch down, we are going to go over everything. I want all this done tonight. No more waiting." I told Joseph.

"I agree." He said walking out of the office. We moved back into the main house because it was more secure than the others. I walked out behind him to find Lilly. When she got back, all she talked about was New Orleans. She went on a Voodoo and a Swamp Tour with the fam. She was talking about going back for Mardi Gras. I was down for a vacation and some fun time with her. I know that we won't be able to do that much when the baby gets here. It was already November and the baby was due in July. Hopefully, everything will be better before then.

Lilly was standing at the stove on the phone. She was asking how much of whatever she was holding had to go into the pot. She started laughing and put the person on speakerphone. "How you not use a measuring when you are cooking, Joel," she asked.

"I don't know. We measure things by how it tastes. If it tastes like it needs more salt you add a little salt. Taste it and tell me what it tastes like." Joel responded. Lilly pulled the spoon out of the pot with some soup looking shit on it. She tasted it and started smacking like she was trying to figure out what was missing.

"Gurl, you know you can't trust Lilly taste buds right now. Her pregnant ass might put cinnamon in that bisque." Another woman said over the phone. I was about to say something when Lilly laughed.

"Shut up, Tyja. I am not that bad." I walked up behind her and hugged her waist. I kissed her on the neck and she moaned loudly.

"Shit, Lilly, what you put in that bisque that got you moaning like that. We are on our way." The lady spoke again.

"It wasn't the bisque crazy ass. It was your brother-in-law Jordan. He is kissing on me and shit. Tell Joel she is going to have to come over here and finished this Corn Shrimp and Crab Bisque. I don't know what I'm doing over here." Lilly said turning around and kissing me on my neck. I needed that pussy bad. When she got home, I took her fast and hard. I wanted to take things nice and slow this time.

"Alright, Lilly, we will be over there in a minute. Jason is on his way over there as well. Tell them none of that fighting shit. We are moving forward and leaving all that other bullshit behind us. Love you, sis, and I'll see you soon." Joel said and hung up. I didn't want to think about that nigga right now. I have been calling him to let him know that there was a hit on our parents. Pops didn't want us to call Ma and tell her, because he said that she needed a quiet vacation as well. She dealt with a lot of shit with my dad being the man that he was. Shit, she been dealing with this her whole life. He hasn't been able to take her on any vacation because of how busy he was. When he saw how quickly she jumped at the idea of going with Joel and Jason, he was happy that it was going to be with their sane baby boy. But at the same time, I needed that nigga.

I couldn't find Roland or Roc for shit, but I knew Jason would have found them. He was going to rip them muthafuckers apart when he found out about the hit that they had on my parents. I looked down at Lilly and pulled her from the stove. I was trying to kiss her, but she dodged me.

"You heard that. No fighting. Ma-Ma has been in a good mood. Don't ruin it with all that shit y'all got going on." Lilly said to me. I couldn't promise her shit. Jason wasn't a forgiving as nigga.

JJ walked in and straight to the stove. He grabbed a spoonful of the soup and put it in his mouth. "It needs a little more salt and pepper." He said while grabbing the salt and pepper. He sprinkled some in there and tasted it again. "Yeah, that the shit Lilly. Pops is going to be happy as fuck. This is his favorite dish." He walked to the door and yelled Pops' name. "Oh Pops! Come see what Lilly cooked." He yelled out twice more, until one of our soldiers came into the room.

"Yo, Pops left with four guards about an hour and forty-five minutes ago. He hasn't come back yet."

I stepped away from Lilly. "Did he tell anyone where he was going?" I asked Vance.

He shook his head no.

"Pops don't tell us shit when he leaves the house." He was right about that.

When we asked that fool about where he was or going, he looked at us like we were stupid. I'm pretty sure that he would have shot Vance if he would have asked.

"Pops knows that we are at war with these bitches. He can't be leaving without telling nobody where he's going. I'm telling Mama on his ass. He will listen then." JJ said.

I pulled out my phone to call him, but was interrupted when Jason walked in. I'm not going to lie. Joel looked like she was serving that pussy on the platter for this nigga. He walked in this bitch glowing like a pregnant woman. He smiled at everybody and spoke.

"What's up y'all?" He said. Lilly walked out of my arms and walked over to Jason. She gave him a hug and kissed him on his cheek.

"Nothing. I just finished making that bisque that Joel made when we were in New Orleans. Do you want to try some?"

"Hell yeah. Did you make biscuits too? That shit was fiya together." He said walking to the stove and moving a stunned JJ out of the way.

"Nigga, what is wrong with you. Give me the damn spoon." Jason told JJ. He snatched the spoon out of JJ's hand and fixed him a bowl.

"No, I didn't make them. Tyja and Joel are on their way here. Tyja will fix them when she gets here." Joseph hearing Tyja's name brought him out of his stun state.

"Hold up. My chocolate baby is here in Philly." Lilly nodded her head yes. JJ hugged Jason and kissed that nigga on his cheek. Jason pushed JJ off of him and wiped his face.

"Man, what the hell is wrong with you?" Jason asked JJ.

JJ started smiling. "You brought me back a souvenir." We all started laughing at this fool. Even though he hasn't said anything to me, somehow, I felt like that nigga was ok now. He looked calm and at peace. I know that there was some shit still bothering him about what happened between us. But, with him walking in here without grilling or attacking me, shows that he wasn't the Jason that I was preparing for.

All three of us was talking about random shit. No business shit. Just brothers talking about family. He was telling us about starting a family with Joel after JJ and I take care of the shit I started. He was still excluding himself from the business. He looked at me and nodded his head.

"What's been going on?" He asked.

Lilly gave me a kiss and walked out of the kitchen. Me and JJ explained things to him and you could see that Jason was struggling with staying sane. This nigga was doing some breathing exercise with his head down. When he looked up, he asked where Pops and Ma were. I told him that Ma was upstairs and we didn't know where Pops was at. Jason jumped up to call Ma, but Pops walked through the back door.

"Sons, what's going on?" He said with bags of shit in his hand.

"Yo, you know that there is a hit on you, and you shopping and shit. Pops, you gotta take this shit more seriously." JJ said to him while reaching for the bags. Pops waved off what JJ was saying. He looked up at Jason and smiled.

"I see that you had a great time in New Orleans." He said to him. Jason shook his head and smiled. "It was alright." He told him, still smiling at Pops' comment.

"Just alright, huh." My father said as Joel and another woman walks into the kitchen. Jason made eye contact with her and his smile got wider. JJ jumped in front of them and introduced himself to the woman.

"I heard that you were my mother's other daughter-in-law. Since I'm the only single son left, I guess we need to start making them wedding plans." He said to the woman. Unlike the reaction he got from Joel, this woman ate that shit up.

"You are right. The wedding is going to be down south, though. My people not balling like that. They can't afford to buy a plane ticket on short notice." She said and turned to Joel. "We should have a double wedding and get it over with, what you think?"

"I don't know, Tyja. My fiancé' don't do crowds. Something nice and simple would be good for us. Right baby." Joel said, walking over to Jason and wrapping her arms around him. He kissed her on the lips and wrapped his arms around her waist. He looked down at her with the same love my father has for my mother. It was something that we all craved as men. We hoped that we would find someone to balance us. Here it is we all got what we wanted. Not everything. We still have to deal with this bullshit I created.

"It's whatever you want, El." Jason replied to her.

I interrupted they little connection. "Hey, enough of all that shit. Y'all had a whole week of that bullshit. Can we get back to business?" I told them.

Jason looked at me over Joel's head. She was staring at me with disgust. She was probably still salty about our conversation back at the house, but that shit would have to take a backseat. If she was going to be with Jason, she would have to know that Jason was who he was and changing him wasn't an option.

"I'm still not killing for this family, bruh. You fucked up big, nigga. I'm just here to make sure that my parents and brother don't fall victim to your greed and bullshit." He said to me nonchalantly. I was about to reply when Lilly stepped in looking confused.

"What is he talking about Jordan? What have you been up to that got the family in this shit?" My family looked at me and shook their heads. I grabbed Lilly's hand and walked us to the bedroom. Another conversation I wasn't ready to have but was forced to do, thanks to Jason. This muthafucker was always fucking shit up.

TWENTY-FOUR

JASON

We watched as Jordan walked Lilly out of the kitchen. That nigga used to brag about how he tells Lilly everything and that they didn't have any secrets in their relationship. Clearly, his ass been lying, and he had to prepare himself for disappointing another person that trusted him.

"Hi, Mr. Jordan, I am Tyja, your new daughter-in-law." Tyja broke the silence with her cheerful introduction. My father couldn't do nothing but laugh. Joel and Tyja were different in many ways. Whatever Joel lacked in, Tyja made up with her laughter and joking mood.

She always had us laughing at some stupid, random shit. I asked her why was her relationship with Tyja so important. She smiled and told me that with all of the ugliness in the world, you have to surround yourself with positive people. People that don't only see the negative in people, but good as well. She said that, that type of behavior can rub off on the most lethal person. I didn't know if she was referring to me or her. But, what I do know is that there was truth behind her words. I felt myself changing for the best.

My father grabbed Tyja in a hug and spoke to her. "Thank God his mother found you for him, because the hoes he brought here had us all wondering." Joel and Tyja looked at Pops in shock.

I bust out laughing with JJ. Joel walked to the stove to continue cooking the food that Lilly was cooking and made a couple of side dishes with it. Tyja and Joseph started talking to each other while she prepared the biscuits. Ma walked in and gave us all a hug and kiss. You can tell that, whatever she was feeling before I got here, was gone.

We all brought the food to the dining room and placed it on the table. Lilly and Jordan walked in quietly. You can tell that she has been crying. Joel pushed her seat over to make room for her. Lilly sat down with a forced smile. Joel glared at Jordan like she wanted to rip that nigga's head off. Ma made a noise to gather everyone's attention.

"I know that our family has been rocky lately. But we are family and that is the way it is. We stand together no matter what. Boys, to build a family of your own, you will have to be the man that your family can trust. No more lies. No more secrets. Understand." Jordan looked at me and nods. He stood and smirked at the family.

"Well, since honesty is something that this family is all about, let's be honest. Pops, why do you feel that Jason has to change who he is, when you created him to be the man that the Stand would fear?" He asked Pops outright.

Pops' smiled dropped. He didn't understand where this question was going or what Jordan was trying to get from the answer. Pops and I made peace with his decision a long time ago. So, for Jordan to bring this shit up now, right after the peace talk Ma spoke, made us think that he wasn't looking for peace in the family.

Ma put her plate down before fixing it and looked at the other women surrounding the table. Joel kissed me on my forehead and got up with the rest of the women to leave the dining area. I stood up with JJ to move the table from Pops and Jordan. Even though the shit was about me, it was between them two.

"Say what you gotta say, nigga. And you better make sure that it is everything you gotta say. Because this conversation will not be had again." My father stood and said to Jordan. I gotta give it to Jordan. He was standing his ground. He looked my father in his eyes and spoke his mind.

"You sent Jason off to be trained as this assassin and when we need him to be just that, it's a problem. I led with what you gave me to lead with. My brothers are supposed to be with me. But they second guess what I do because you taught them differently from what you have shown me. In the meetings, you always have the last say, the last words. Now, when I sit in the meeting, these old fucks try to tell me what I can't have and why I can't have it. I shouldn't have to ask for shit. This is ours." Jordan replied with that same shit he told me and JJ at the house. This is why I tried to stay away from Jordan. He never did see the bigger picture. Pops walked up to Jordan and stood toe to toe with him.

"I wasn't showing you how powerful I can be over the other men in the Stand, Jordan. I was showing you how respecting others can gain the respect of many. You missed that lesson because you were too busy planning a takeover then. The fear that these men have in Jason wasn't brought on by his last name alone. But, by the work he put in. He gained that respect. You think that because he is your brother and I am your father that it should be given to you without the work. Yea, you seriously got the game fucked up." JJ and I shook our head at Jordan.

How can he not get this? I didn't have to be in a meeting to see what Pops was telling Jo. He showed us that shit in his daily activities.

Jordan looked like he still didn't understand what Pops was talking about. And at this point, I was tired of listening to this shit. I didn't have a high level of patience for stupidity, neither did JJ. I could feel his irritation boiling over. Jordan stepped back from Pops and looked over at us.

"How do y'all want to handle this situation then?" He said not really giving us a choice in the matter. He was battling with trying to do what Pops want and what he been feeling his whole life.

"It's only one way to go Jordan and you made sure of that. All we have to do is eliminate the Browns. If we do that, the other men in the Stand won't have the resources to come at us," JJ replied. I disagreed with all this shit.

"Man, you sound stupid as fuck. There is no way you should trust a muthafucker that stood or plotted against you. Think JJ. Jordan murdered these men sons. You don't think that even without the resources Brown have, that they will stop coming for this family. They are hurting, nigga. You wouldn't break bread with a man that has any of our blood on their hands. Why would they? Take all them fools out and start all over." I told them. My father nodded in agreement.

"That's right, we got to remove them all. But that's only if they are in this with Roland. He has been trying to take over for the longest. We have to find this out for sure. If so, then we will have to kill them all, including Derrick." I knew it must have hurt him to say that shit. Derrick was with him in the beginning.

"So, Jason, let us know what you need to take Roc and Roland out. We will deal with the rest of the Brown crew. Tee Glen is coming down here with Tank and the others." Jordan said that shit so casually. This muthafucker thought he was slick. "I already told you I ain't doing that shit, bruh. You better call for the Elites." I turned to walk away, and this fool grabbed my arm.

"The fuck you mean call for the Elites. Why do that when we got you?" Jordan replied. See what I'm saying. That nigga heard what he wants to hear.

"Nigga you don't got me. That's what you not understanding. Everybody is so easy to forgive the shit you have done, but I can't. You used me nigga. That dark shit eats me alive every day and night and you used that for your gain. I told you before, I'm not taking orders from you, nigga." I told him, getting in his face.

Jo was another muthafucker pushing at my buttons. It was clear that he didn't want me to change. And I was pretty sure that I was about to relapse on his ass. It's been two almost three weeks without me killing someone. That was a record for me. I was used to making four kills a week. But, I started feeling that familiar twitch in my hands. I wanted to hit this bitch so bad, but I knew that, if I did this time, I was going to follow through and kill this nigga. Ma walked in and told us that Tee Glen was here.

"You don't have to announce me Joyce. These niggas should feel my presence in this bitch. What y'all up here booted up fa." Tee Glen said to us. She always had a way with making an entrance. Jordan and I was still in a standoff when she walked up to us. "I know y'all muthafuckers heard me." I turned and looked at her.

My Teedie looked just like Ma. She was taller than her and liked to wear different color wigs. Today she had on a short black and burgundy one. I smiled and brought her into a hug. She hugged me back and laughed.

"Are you good, boy?" She asked me, with her hands on my face. I haven't seen her and my cousin in years. I tell her what I have been telling everyone else. This time it was the truth.

"I am good Teedie." She smiled and gripped my jaws tightly with a gun underneath my chin.

"That's good Jason. Because, if I hear anyone tell me that you went postal on my sister again, I will kill you myself." She told me seriously.

"Yes, Teedie." I told her and pulled her into another hug. Tank and Tristian walked into the kitchen and greeted my father. They spoke to JJ and stared at me.

"Ah Jason, do you remember the time when I got you that Rambo knife for Christmas? You told me that you were going to owe me for that one. Well, if you spare my life, you won't have to owe me shit after that. I mean for life." Tristan told me.

Tee Glen walked up to him and slapped him on the back of his head. "Shut yo stupid ass up. Jason ain't killing nobody in here." Tristan laughed uncertainly. Tank walked up to me with his hand out. I was mad at this nigga too. He let Jordan suck him into this greed shit. The Stand down south was already disbanded. But like I told Jordan, that's their mess to clean up.

"You good." I told him, ignoring his hand. I wasn't going to pretend shit with nobody. The rest of the women walked in and Tristan and Tank's mouths dropped.

"Naw, nigga, stop drooling over our women. Before y'all really get fucked up." JJ told them while walking towards Tyja. Joel walked to me and pulled me by my ears. I didn't know why that shit turned me on, but it did.

"You need to eat. Let me fix everyone a plate and y'all can discuss this over dinner." She told me. My Tee Glen walked towards us and I knew that she was about to size Joel up.

"And who is you." She asked all ghetto and shit. Joel turned around and smiled at her.

"Hey Tee Glen, I am Joel. Jason told me so much about you and your cooking. You have to tell me about that lasagna that be having these niggas Crip walking in here." I draped my arms around Joel and kissed her on the top of her head. My Tee Glen looked at us and started smiling.

"I'll give you whatever you want, if you keep my nephew happy." She said and grabbed Joel's hand to help her fix plates with Ma and Tyja. Lilly was fixing the drinks and grabbing the silverware.

"Oh shit, nigga. Is that Joel?" Tank asked a still pissed off Jordan. Jordan looked over at us and shook his head.

"Yeah, that's her." He said and walked out of the kitchen.

The night continued with more introductions. We ate while Tank told us how he took over the stand in the ATL. My Teedie cursed him and Tristan ass out like this was her first time hearing this story. Pops and JJ told her Jordan's side and she got madder. Lilly got up from the table when the subject changed to how irresponsible Jordan was being. I felt bad for her. She really didn't sign up for this bullshit.

"So now that everything is out the bag, what is our next step? I know Roland is going to keep his family in hiding until the hit is done or until all the Davis crew is gone. We need to come up with a plan and execute that shit with no errors." Teedie told us.

I sat and listened while everyone talked about how they were going to solve this problem. I got up and went into the other room. I never sat in the meeting when they were planning shit like this before. It doesn't make sense for me to do it now. I sat on the couch and turned on the TV. Joel and Tyja walked in and sat next to me.

"Don't feel like watching no football, Jason. Let's put on a movie." Tyja said and snatched the remote out of my hand.

"Look, don't be snatching shit in here. I wanna watch the game. Carry your ass up in JJ room and watch whatever." I told her ass. She poked her tongue out at me and continued changing the channels. My phone started ringing and I pulled it out to answer. It was an unknown number. I got up and walked outside to answer it. "Who this?"

"I need a picture of the chick, Mya. She has been using a fake name, birthday, and social security number." Dex told me. I knew this bitch had to be somebody else. She knew too much about my family to be some regular chick. I didn't do social medias or any other shit that would have my shit on display like that.

"Aight, I got you," I told Dex. I hung up the phone and walked back into the house. Lilly was sitting on the couch with Joel and Tyja.

"Are you good?" Joel asked me. I grabbed her hand and brought her to my bedroom. She sat on the bed and waited for my answer.

"I found it strange that Mya knew my mother's real name and what you have been doing for the family. I ain't the pillow talking type of nigga. So, I was trying to figure out who she really was. I sent the shit to my contact and he told me that she was using a fake name. I gotta get a picture of her to send to him." I explained to her. I didn't want to leave her in the dark.

She pulled out her phone and started typing something. My phone went off again and it was a message from her. I opened it up and it was a picture of Mya and the three girls she was with.

"Where did you get this from?" I asked, now suspicious of her.

"Don't look at me like that? The girls that she was hanging with looked familiar. Since Tyja be around the city a lot, I took the picture to ask her about them. She has never seen Mya, but the girls that were behind her, stay around Tyja people house in the seventh ward in New Orleans." Joel told me.

I sent the picture to Dex and put my phone back in my pocket. "You need to go back in there to see what they are discussing." Joel said to me. She wrapped her arms around my waist and was staring up at me.

"Naw, I'm not doing that Joel." I told her shaking my head.

"Jason, you don't want to be kept in the dark. You need to know what you are up against. If Tee Glen knows Roland and his family, you can get some information from her to protect the family better." She said and kissed me on the lips. "That's why we are here, correct," she said to me.

I dropped my head back and let out a sigh. I could have easily got the information from Dex, but I wanted all his attention on the Mya situation. But, I do hate it when she makes sense. I looked back down at her and gave her a kiss. She grabbed my hand and walked us back downstairs. I stood in front of the kitchen door, not wanting to go in. She pushed me in and called me a baby. I sat down in the chair and listened.

TWENTY-FIVE

JORDAN

We have been at it for weeks now. We didn't just take out Roland's businesses but his friends and family as well. Anybody that was related to Roland or his wife got bodied. Everyone that must have meant something to them was probably with them, because it still didn't bring them out of hiding. We were able to get back all of the shit that was stolen from us out of Roland's warehouse.

That wasn't enough for me.

I wanted them niggas to bleed for this hide and go seek bullshit. I was out every night with the crew. Lilly and I have been arguing about any and everything. I can feel myself changing with every kill I made. The shit they were trying to keep Jason from, I was feeling now. The shit was addictive. We were on our way to take out Roland's wife's parents. We got word that they were not in hiding with the rest of his family. I was feeling the adrenaline for this kill. I wanted to take my time and torture them. My hands started sweating and I felt my body rocking.

"Yo Jo, you alright cousin. You look like a fiend over there." Tank said to me.

"I just want to kill them all." I told him calmly. I couldn't explain to him how I was really feeling. It was something that couldn't be explained.

"Jo, you sound just like Jason over there. Look, the crew can do the parents in. We can go back to the house and chill for a minute." I looked at that nigga to see if he was serious or not.

"If you turn this car around, I will stab you in the throat." I told him while taking my knife out and placing it on the dashboard.

Tank looked at me like I lost all my marbles. He continued driving to the house without another word. When we got there, I grabbed my knife, got out, and went to the front door of the house. Tristan already sent us the floor plans for the house. So, I pretty much knew where I was going when I got in. I kicked the door down and headed to their bedroom with Tank following behind me. Everyone else broke off to search the rest of the house.

I walked in and pulled my knife out. I stood over the man twirling my knife. The man woke up and saw me. He reached for the gun in the nightstand, but I grabbed his hand and sawed it off. His screams woke his wife up. Tank put a gun in her face and told her to be quiet. The man was holding onto his arm with blood leaking everywhere.

"I am going to ask you once. Where is Roland?" I said. He looked up at me and shook his head. I was hoping that he didn't answer. I was going to kill him anyway but at least I didn't have to hear no bullshit before doing it. I grabbed him by his hair and slit his throat. The woman started crying again and Tank shot her in the face. I walked out of the bedroom and out the front door. Tank and the others followed me out. They stood there waiting for other instructions.

"Go home, we will meet up at the center tomorrow." I told them and jumped in the car. Tank stood out there discussing whatever with them and got in the car with me. He drove us through the gate of our home and pulled into the garage. I sat in the car to prepare myself for the nagging Lilly was about to do. Tank was staring at me still.

"What you gotta say, Tank?" I told him. I hate when muthafuckers stare and shit.

"Tristan said that some of Roland's family members will be rolling in later this week. That will give us more time to plan things out." He told me. I knew that he was lying to me. I got the same intel he did. His people was coming in tomorrow night. I didn't feel like arguing with him, so I dapped him off and went inside. You can smell the food throughout the house. I stuck my head in the kitchen and the women were at it like always. I turned and went into the office. Pops was talking to Tristan and Joseph while Jason was sitting there.

Jason and Joel never left after that night. He sat in the meetings and didn't say shit. He was really getting on my fucking nerves. This shit would have been over with if that nigga would have done what he was supposed to do. JJ fell in line and killed off a couple of people to get to Roland while Jason was up in here doing shit.

"What did you get, son?" Pops said breaking me out of my thoughts. I walked to the bar and fixed myself a drink. I went through at least three bottles a day. It was another thing that me and Lilly argued about. She just didn't know how the liquor was holding me together at this point.

"Nothing," I told him and took my drink.

"I found out the other day that it is Roland behind this shit. The other members don't have anything to do with it. So, all we gotta do is take out the Browns." I heard my father say. At this point, I wanted all of them muthafuckers dead.

"Hey Tristan, can you give us a minute." JJ asked. Tristan got up and left the office without any questions. Pops walked to the bar and grabbed my shoulder.

"Son," he asked me. I looked up at him confused. He was approaching me like he did Jason when he was falling off.

"I'm good, Pops. I just want this to be over with." I told him truthfully.

"We all do, Jordan." JJ said to me.

"Not all of us," I told them while looking at Jason. He smirked at me and that had me seeing red all over again. I went to charge at him, but my Pops and JJ held me back.

"Who you smiling at, bitch?" I told him. This nigga looked like he wasn't fazed by nothing I was saying. He stood, and the smirk on his face became a wide smile. He was baiting me in and I was falling for it. I pushed JJ and Pops off me and tackled that bitch through the door. I got up and got tackled again by Tank this time.

"Calm yo mutha fucking ass down, nigga." I saw JJ coming out of the office with Pops. They all were holding me down now. The women came out of the kitchen to see what was going on. Lilly came over and started beating on Tank's back.

"Get your fucking hands off him," she yelled and cried out.

"Lilly stop that! Joel and Tyja get Lilly. Bring her ass to the room." My mom said. Joel and Tyja grabbed her and carried her out of the room.

"Get off of me," I told them.

"Calm down first, son. We will let you up when you calm down." Pops told me. I dropped my head to the floor and relaxed. They let me go one by one. I got up and looked around the room. Everyone was staring like I was some rabid dog. Jason was leaning against the wall with that same smirk on his face. I was about to approach him again when Ma jumped in front of him. I can see him moving towards me now without the smile.

"Jo, go and check on Lilly." Ma said to me. I shook my head and was about to move around her. She grabbed my face and looked at me.

"Tre' do what yo Momma say. Go check on your babies." She said, using my nickname.

I looked at her and nodded. I walked out of the room and went upstairs. I got to the door when I heard the women talking.

"Lilly, you have to calm down. The baby can feel when you are stressing yourself out and shit." Tyja told her.

"I'm trying you guys. He just been acting so different now. He is always angry and drinking. I don't know if I can take this anymore." Lilly cried out.

I stood there and listened to her talk. I knew that I was changing for the worse and the only thing that would change that will be the heads of the men on the Stand.

"Lilly, if you think being here is going to stress you out even more, leave. You can go to your parents or go to New Orleans to live in my house. Shit, we will come with you until all this shit is over with." Joel said to her. I wasn't having that shit. I opened the door and walked in.

"Get the fuck out." I told them. Tyja held up her hands and walked out the room. Joel looked at me and stood where she was. Lilly grabbed her hand and told her that it was ok.

"Love you, sis." She told Lilly and walked out.

"You want to leave," I asked her. She stared at me and ignored me. "DO YOU WANT TO LEAVE!" I yelled at her. She started crying and shaking her head. "Good! There is no place that Joel can put you. I will always find you and drag yo ass right back here where you belong. Fuck with it if you want." I turned towards the door. "Lay yo ass down." I told her before walking out of the door.

I went back downstairs to confront Joel about the bullshit she was saying. She was still in my fucking business. I walked into the kitchen and she was talking to Joseph. I didn't see Jason nowhere. It didn't matter. I approached her and JJ to say what I had to say.

"Yo, mind your fucking business. I don't want you in my girl ear saying shit she don't need to hear. She ain't going no fucking where. Keep telling her that shit and you will be the one gone, bitch." I told Joel.

JJ jumped in front of me. "Aw, man, chill ou-"

"Nah, Joseph. I got this." She told him.

JJ stepped back and let Joel step forward. She looked up at me and I swear that I was looking at a completely different person. "You see Jordan, I'm not some weak ass girl that you can scare when you raise your voice. I can be that Bitch that would go toe to toe with you in any mood you in muthafucker. Now excuse me, maybe I didn't hear you right." She said getting in my face. The look she was giving me had me rethinking shit. "Did you just threaten me, Jordan?"

Tyja got up from the seat she was watching us in. She grabbed

Joel's hand and tried pulling her out of my face. "Joel, let it go sis. Leave it alone." Joel kept eyes on me while ignoring Tyja pulling on her.

"Nah, fuck that Tyja, this nigga looks like he got something else to say. Say it nigga, but you better mean it this time." She told me. Jason walked into the room and pulled both of them back.

"This what you do nigga. You can't get at me, so you go after my girl. You a bitch fa that." Jason said, getting in my face. I was still stunned by the shit I saw in Joel. She was still looking at me with Tyja pulling her out of the room.

"Yo J, I don't think Joel needed your help man." Tank said on the side of me. I looked around and saw that everyone was in the kitchen. Ma looked more relieved for me than Joel. I walked around Jason to go out the back door.

"Tell yo girl to mind her business."

TWENTY-SIX
JASON

I was about to follow his ass out the door, but JJ grabbed me.

"Trust me nigga when I say, Joel handled her business. That nigga looked like he seen a ghost." JJ told me. I wasn't listening to that shit though. Joel should never have to defend herself especially from my brother. I can see the changes in him. He was becoming uncontrollable. I'm pretty sure he was out there right now looking for somebody to kill, since no one around here wasn't taking his shit.

Tyja walked back into the kitchen without Joel.

"She's good J, she went to use the bathroom." I made a detour and headed to the bathroom. I needed to see it for myself. I don't know if Jordan scared her or not. But, if he did, I was going to fuck him up fa real. I got to the bathroom and twisted the knob. It didn't open, so I started knocking.

"Open this door, Joel."

"Give me a minute, baby." She said through the door.

"No minutes, El. Open this door before I knock this bitch down." I said backing up to kick the damn door down. I heard the door being unlocked and it opened. She was standing there drying off her hands.

"I can't use the bathroom now." I snatched her ass up and pulled her to me.

"You good, El." I asked her while looking into her eyes. She stared up at me and nodded her head.

"I'm good babe. Jordan don't scare me. That shit was nothing compared to what I saw in your eyes." She grabbed my face to make sure I understand what she was about to say. "Don't worry about it." She told me and began to rub on my temples.

That shit makes me feel so relaxed and calm. She does this to me every night and I wake up the next morning without the nightmares. She kissed me on my nose and told me that it was time to eat. We walked back into the kitchen and everyone was taking the food into the dining room. I sat down and started eating the food that Joel fixed. Joel and Tyja went upstairs to eat with Lilly. I finished eating and went up to my room. I called Dex to see if he got any information on Mya and he told me not yet. I took a shower and fell asleep waiting on Joel.

I woke up the next morning without Joel. I don't remember her coming in at all last night. I went into the bathroom to take care of my hygiene. I threw on a shirt with my Nike slides and went looking for her. When I got to the kitchen Jo, JJ, and Tank were eating. Ma and Tee Glen were standing at the island looking at baby magazines and shit.

"Ma, where is Joel."

"Joel and Tyja went to Lilly's doctor's appointment. She finds out what she is having today." She said smiling.

"Wait," I turned to Jordan. "Why yo punk ass here? Why didn't you go to see about your seed nigga?" His ass was sitting there frowning and shit.

"Because they want to have some fucking baby reveal party. I don't want that shit. Ma told me to stay my ass here until they get back." He said stuffing his food in his mouth.

"Aye Jo, whatever you got against my girl, you talk to me about that. Don't address my girl while I ain't around, nigga." I told that fool straight up. I knew Joel wanted me to leave the shit alone. I just had to let his ass know that the shit wasn't cool. He nodded his head and continued eating. I grabbed me a plate of food and sat at the island. Pops came through that bitch like his ass was on fire.

"I'll be right back." He told us and kissed Ma on the lips.

"Pops, man, where yo ass going. You can't be leaving like this." JJ told him. Pops turned and looked at me.

"I gotta take care of something right quick."

"Take some people with you, Senior, before you give your boys a heart attack." Ma told Pops.

"Alright, I'll take Luke and a couple of other men with me." He said walking out the door.

"Take Bruiser, Pops." I yelled. Pops looked back at me and smiled.

When the back door was closed, JJ got up and approached Ma.

"Damn, Ma, how you gonna let him leave like that?"

Ma looked up at JJ and started laughing with Tee Glen. "Boy if you don't sit yo ass down somewhere. Yo Daddy is a grown ass man."

"With a grown ass woman. When he talks about leaving like that, you need to shut that shit down, Ma. His ass going straight to the shopping mall to get some more stuff for the baby." JJ said mad as fuck fa real.

Jo and Tank started laughing at this fool. "JJ shut that shit up. You just be mad that Pops didn't take you with him." Jordan said to him.

"Fa real, though. He going to buy all the good shit." JJ said and walked out of the kitchen. Everyone was laughing but me. The look my father gave me had me thinking about where he was really going.

TWENTY-SEVEN

JORDAN SR

Yeah, I know what y'all thinking. I fucked up letting Jordan run the empire. Jason didn't want it and Joseph wasn't ready. I thought that if I gave him a little more attention that he would have got out of that selfishness and do what I taught him. Jordan has always wanted things his way. We talked about these plans before he took over. He asked why we had to share everything that our family worked so hard for. I tried to teach him that it was us against them and that greed was one of the main reasons why black-owned businesses couldn't have anything. Instead of supporting each other, we find ways to take each other out and tear each other down. If that wasn't the case, you had the other type. The ones that were sitting on the throne and didn't want to help others that was struggling to get their paper right.

Lil Jordan didn't want to hear that. He was determined to put him and his brothers on a throne above all. Don't get me wrong, his idea was good; he was just doing the shit the wrong way. But the truth of the matter was, I wanted my family back together. Me and Jason's relationship has always been different from Joseph and Jordan. I was the reason why Jason was the way he was. I noticed the change in him when he was six. The boys were playing around with some kids at the park. Joseph had a basketball and one of the older kids were trying to take it from him. Jordan and Jason saw what was going on and went to check on their brother. The older boy pushed JJ down and kicked him before they made it to him. Jordan went to check on JJ, while Jason ran the boy down. He jumped on the boy and beat the shit out of him.

The guards that were with them couldn't pull Jason off of the boy, until Joyce was in his sight. He looked up at his mother like she was the flashlight in a dark room. When he got home, he told me what happened and how he felt. I put him with Lavell, who was one of my other close friends back then. He taught him how to control and channel that anger. Jason got quicker, stronger, and became one lethal killer at the age of fourteen. He has been killing for this family for a long time. I could have led him down a better path, but this was something that Jason was good at.

When I see him now, I regret my decisions that I made for him. He has Joel, which was true, but I didn't want that to be the only reason for his sanity. He should be able to control that shit now. I thought that sending him to the Navy would change that. Jordan was right. It did make my boy worse. Jason and I already discussed what I have done, and he forgave me. I just felt like I had to do more.

I was sitting in my office and looking over some of my contacts. I went to a meeting a couple of weeks ago with five other members of the Stand. Everyone was telling me how Roland was going around telling everyone that we were finished. I told them after everything was done with this Roland shit, that we were going to sit down and talk. They all agreed and ended the meeting. I was talking to Derrick when my cell phone started beeping. I read the message that was sent and told Derrick that I was going to call him back. I got up to lock my office door. I sat down and dialed the number that texted me.

"Hello this is Jordan Sr.," I answered.

"Hi, Mr. Jordan I didn't have anyone else to call." The woman said on the other end.

"Calm down sweetheart. Tell me your name." I asked her.

"Mya," she cried out.

"Ok, Mya, tell me what happened."

"I was coming out of the grocery store and two men grabbed me and tried to put me in a van. I yelled out for help and a crowd of people came to my rescue. They let me go but told me that they were going to kill me and my bastard. After that, they were going for Jason. I don't know what to do." She told me.

"Did you tell Jason that you were pregnant?" I asked her.

"Yes, I told him weeks ago. He told me to abort it, because he was afraid that the baby would come out like him. I'm scared that if he sees me, he will kill me. Can you please help me?" Maya says over the phone. I knew what she was saying was true. Jason told me on many of occasions that he didn't want any children. I was hoping that he would have changed his mind. It looks like he hasn't if he had threatened this woman.

"He is ok, right now. We can sit him down and talk about this together. Would that be ok?" I said while grabbing my keys and jacket.

"Yes, sir, but only if you come and get me. I don't trust no one else." She told me.

"Text me your address. I am on my way to you."

"Ok, I am texting you right now. He told me that you were the only man he trusts right now. So, I am putting my trust in you Mr. Jordan. I heard that your sons can be just as ruthless as Jason. He told me that they will do anything he says. I don't know if he told them to kill me on sight as well." She told me.

"I don't think that will happen. I will talk to Jason and the boys about this. Just pack a few things so that I can bring you here with us to explain everything."

I hung up the phone and walked out of my office. I went into the kitchen where everybody was eating.

"I'll be right back." I said. I kissed my wife and looked at my sons.

"Pops, man, where yo ass going? You can't be leaving like this." JJ said, sounding like the parent. I looked over at Jason and told them that I was going to take care of something. Joyce asked me to take a few men with me. I'll take Luke and a couple of other men with me. Jason yelled for me to take Bruiser. I smiled at him and walked out the door.

Hopefully, this would be a better decision made for his life than the one I made a long time ago. I jumped in my truck with Luke, and Bruiser was with the other men in the truck behind me. I gave Luke the address and he punched it in the GPS. We began to drive towards the address and I was feeling some way about this whole situation.

I reached for my phone to call Jason and stopped myself. I didn't want to trigger nothing in him. Joel wasn't there to keep him calm.

"What's wrong, Senior?" Luke asked. I looked at my friend and told him what was going on.

"I think we should go and get her. Roland is already looking for the upper hand. Especially after hearing the news about his wife's parents."

"I hear what you are saying, Luke. I just don't want Jason to react a certain way." I told him. We continued driving until we came up to the address. I got out of the car with my phone in my hand.

"I gotta call him," I said and dialed Jason's number. It went straight to voicemail. "Son, call me when you get this message." I hung up and tried again. "Shit, voicemail again," I said.

"Why don't you call Joseph phone? He always has it on him." I hung up and dialed JJ's number. Before he can answer, a woman walked out with two bags. Luke went to grab her bags and put them in the back of the trunk. I went to grab her hand and saw that she was showing just like Lilly.

"Do you have everything you need." I asked her

"Yes, Sir." She said without the fear that she had over the phone. I took a good look at her and knew that something wasn't right. I heard JJ screaming hello on the phone.

"Yeah, where is Jason." I asked him while looking at the woman. She was looking around at the men that were with me.

"Yeah, what's up Pops." Jason asked.

"Jason," I said his name loudly so that she can hear me. She put her head down and started rubbing her belly. "Who is Mya?"

Mya picked her head up and smiled at me. She pulled out a gun and placed it in my face.

"He doesn't know who I am." She said to me in a different accent. Bullets started flying and bodies were dropping. Luke got hit in the chest after he took out two men. Bruiser came out of nowhere and tackled Mya to the ground. She let off a shot and it hit me in the shoulder. She then turned the gun on Bruiser and shot him three times in the head. I pulled out my gun and felt someone's gun pressed to the back of my head.

"Hello, Senior. You always had a soft spot for the damsel in distress." Roland said.

"Fuck you, bitch. Do what you gotta do to me cause I ain't telling you shit." I told his punk ass. He motioned for his men to drag me back into that lying bitch's house. They jumped me like some hoes and shot both of my knees out. It didn't matter; I still wasn't giving them shit. After they realized that I wasn't giving in, Roland came around with his gun in my face. The woman was laughing and eating an apple.

"You laughing now, but you better go into Atlantis hiding bitch. Something worse than Jason will be coming for you." I said to her. That stopped her from laughing.

"Any last words Senior." Roc said to me. I looked up at Roland and smiled. "My sons will run all this shit. Because you have just unleashed the devil himself. Good luck with trying to hide from him." I told them all. Everyone in attendance felt them words. I close my eyes and thought of my family, before my life was taken.

TWENTY-EIGHT

JASON

I called Pops' phone back over and over, and it kept going to voicemail.

"Tristan," I yelled for him. I was walking into the office when he came in behind me. "I need you to track my father's phone. Now!" I demanded of him.

"Ok," he replied and got to work. Jo and JJ walked in asking what was wrong. "Pops called me and asked about a girl that I was fucking with before Joel. The bitch followed me to New Orleans and been calling me talking about she was pregnant." Jordan and JJ's mouths dropped. "It ain't mine. She was fucking more than one dude when I was with her. I told my connect to check her out and he told me that she wasn't who I thought she was. Pops just called, asked me about her and the phone disconnected right after that."

I told them while calling Dex for some information. "Tell me something," I told him.

"Shit J, this bitch work for some assassin clan. She has been killing muthafuckers for a long time, man. She was sent down here to take out your family. I am trying to get in their database for a couple of days now and that shit is locked up tight."

"Hey, whoever has Pops smashed his phone along with the others." Tristan said to us.

"Try to break through that shit, Dex. That bitch got my father." I told him. I grabbed my keys and was headed out the front door.

"Jason, where are you going?" JJ said following behind me.

"Her house." He grabbed his jacket and we both walked out the door. When we got to the car, our phone went off. It was a text message from an unknown number. It was pictures of my father, shot up in a chair. I stood there and stared at the pictures until I heard my mother scream.

I ran into the house and went straight to the kitchen. Tee Glen was holding Ma up. JJ went to her and held them both tightly. Jordan came into the kitchen with Tank running behind him.

"This is your fucking fault." He said right before he swung on me. I stumbled back from the hit. I put my head down and listened to him rant.

"It's all your fault. If you would have killed them bitches when I told you, Pops would be still alive. You up in this bitch doing Yoga and finding your inner peace while they were plotting on our parents. Let me go Tank." He yelled over and over. And he was right. If I would have done what I was raised to do, Pops would be here with us. Ma wouldn't be crying her eyes out right now. All this shit was happening because of me. I wanted to be different.

I wanted to change, for her.

Her.

I picked my head up and looked Jordan in his eyes. He stopped fighting Tank and stood there. Everyone was quiet and didn't make a move. They didn't have anything to worry about. They weren't the target. The bitch behind them were.

Joel was standing there with Tyja and Lilly. "What's going on?" Lilly asked. My eyes stayed on Joel. She was trying to read me, but it wasn't going to happen. I walked in Joel's direction with rage. Ma jumped in front of me and faced the woman.

"Senior was murdered today, Joel." She said it quickly.

"No," Lilly said out loud. "That can't be true. He said that he will be here when we get back. I was supposed to tell him that we were having a boy." She cried out. Jordan went to her and held her tightly. Joel walked towards me and I shook my head.

"Stay the fuck away from me." I told her.

The way it came out, stopped her. My mother was trying to calm me down, but right now wasn't the time. Tee Glen came to remove my mother from in front of me. I closed my eyes and felt myself falling in that hell that has been calling me for years.

"Jason," I heard someone call out my name.

I opened up my eyes and Joel was walking towards me again. "If you want to be the first of many, keep coming. I can use you for warm up." I told her.

Joel's back straightened, and her chest was going in and out. She tilted her head to get a better look at me. JJ and Tank told me about the look she gave Jordan, when he made his threats. I guess this was it. Because the way she was looking at me now, had me ready to test her skills that she apparently been hiding.

"Was that a threat?" She asked moving forward.

"Nah, a promise." I told her with a smirk.

"Gud." She said with a devilish smile. Tyja and Lilly jumped in front of Joel. They were trying to talk her down. I took a step forward, but Jordan and JJ jumped in front of me.

"Joel, he is not worth it. Think sis." Tyja told her.

"She is right Joel. Just go. Everything is going to be alright." Lilly said.

"I am here, sis, and I ain't going nowhere." Tyja said the exact same words to her, that she used to keep me sane. Joel looked at Tyja and started shaking her head. "I know, sis, let's go." Tyja told her and pulled on her earlobe. Joel calmed herself and put her head down. She looked up at me with tears falling down her face. The love that was in her eyes the other night was gone. She was looking at me now, regretting everything that we had shared. And I was ok with that. Where I was going, I didn't need to be reminded of that shit.

She turned and walked out of the door. Tyja turned around and looked at me. I don't know what it was about them women from the south. Tyja wasn't afraid at all. She walked up to me with unshed tears in her eyes. "You just made the biggest mistake of your life." Tyja told me and walked out the same door Joel went out of.

My phone started ringing and it was Dex.

"What," I answered.

"I know where they took your father. I also have the locations of the Browns." He told me. I walked around Jordan and JJ.

"Send Jordan and JJ the address to Pops' location. Send me the rest." I said walking out the door. I got into my car and headed to my workshop. I was going to prep for the bodies that I was going torture.

TWENTY-NINE

JORDAN

Five years later

THIS PAST FEW years been rough. After Pops died, Jason went crazy. He called us in to watch him torture Roland and Roc by feeding them to piranhas, piece by piece. He had us in a theater, sitting in the front row, while he sliced them niggas up. JJ and Tank were eating popcorn, yelling out body parts that Jason should cut off next. These niggas were crazy together.

After the Browns were taken out, I asked my brother what they wanted to do next. Jason agreed to kill whoever without questions asked. Jo wanted us to rebuild the Stand like Pops asked. We made a few changes with the rest of the members of the Stand agreeing with everything that I had asked for in the beginning. I looked into some of Roland's businesses and he was partners with some people overseas. Tank and Dex set us up to meet them and discuss further business arrangements. They were all satisfied with us being their new partners and moved forward.

THE WAY TO A KILLER'S HEART   161

Jason was on the hunt for the bitch that set up Pops. Every lead that Dex and Tristan thought they had, led to a dead end. He tried to talk to some of the other assassin's clans about Mya, but no one had information on her. Jason was becoming angrier and more volatile with each kill.

Ma had tried to reach out to him, but he became distant. Dex and Tristan talked to him when there was a job that needed to be done. And that was only through the phone. He had invited JJ and Tank over when he was torturing someone. Jason and I hadn't talked much after Pops' death. The Jason that they were trying to save, was no more. He was completely insane with no conscious.

Ma and Tee Glen had been traveling around the world together. She didn't feel like sitting at home all of the time, and Lilly goes with them every once and a while. Now that she is getting further along with our second child, she has been staying home with our son, Jordan Jr. I was at the car dealership handling some paperwork when my I received a call. I looked down and saw that it was lil guard, Kacey.

"Yo, what up?" I asked shutting off the computer.

"Hey boss, somebody tried to off Lilly and Lil Man." He told me.

"Where the fuck is you?" I yelled out. I signaled for JJ to follow me out to my car.

"We just made it back to the house. She's good boss, all three of them are. There were other men helping us clear out the situation." Kacey replied.

I was getting into the car with JJ. "I am on the way. Lock everything down and don't let no one in until I get there." I told him and hung up the phone. I peeled off and headed home to my family. This shit cannot be happening, bruh.

"Nigga, What's goin on?" Jo asked.

"Them muthafuckers went after Lilly and Jr., bruh. After my fucking kid, nigga." I yelled. JJ hopped on the phone and called Jason and put him on speaker.

"Speak," this nigga's voice was dark as fuck.

"They came after nephew." JJ told him. I didn't know how he would react to that. He had seen Jr. only three times since he was born.

"On the way," he responded and then hung up.

"Them niggas must not know that Jason's head had been fucked up for a while now." JJ said, shaking his head.

"They already know that shit, JJ. That nigga been making all types of noise since Pops died. So, you know the niggas that came after my son and wife must really want it, knowing that Jason is coming after them." I told JJ. This was something that we had to worry about.

I almost ran over the gate to get to my house. I jumped out the car barely throwing it in park. I ran inside, and Jason was sitting with Lilly and JoJo. He was listening to my animated ass son talking about some movie that he saw and was afraid of.

"So, are you going to get him. Momma said that you were the best at getting rid of monsters. I don't like being scared Uncle Jason." JoJo told Jason. Jason leaned forward with dark eyes and responded seriously to him.

"When you see that nigga again, tell him that I'm gonna fuck him up, nice and slow."

JoJo smiled and threw his arms around him. Jason didn't know how to react to that. He pat Jr. on the head like he was a fucking dog. Jason looked up at me and turned my son around to face me.

"Daddy," JoJo yelled and ran towards me. I held out my arms and caught my son. Lilly got up and ran to me with anger in her eyes.

"Are you ok?" I asked her.

"Fuck no, I ain't alright. These niggas came after me and our son Jordon. I mean, what the fuck? I had to bust at them niggas to keep them from following us." She told me angrily. She had also changed after Pops died. She had been handling this shit with the fam and business with ease now. She was becoming a real boss chick, hanging around with Ma and Tee Glen.

Before we can ask any more questions, Tank came in with Tristan. "Hey, Derrick called and told us that someone tried to kill his other son, Dorian while he was at school. The Stand has called a meeting and wants Jason to come with us. They said that they have some information for him." Tank told us. I looked at Lilly and she was already gathering Jr. up to go to one of the safe houses. I'm pretty sure that she called Ma about what happened. Ma was about to be in the streets with us shooting these niggas up, too.

I made sure that Lilly and Jr were in the car before we pulled off. I was sitting in the backseat with Jason, while JJ and Tank sat in the front. This nigga was looking straight ahead, like at the back of the passenger seat. He was mumbling shit under his breath and shaking his head. JJ looked back and started talking to him like he understood what he was saying.

"Why it doesn't seem right, J?"

He started mumbling some other shit, and JJ was nodding his head in agreement. Tank looked back at me for some kind of translation. I hunched my shoulders at his ass. I didn't know what them fools were talking about.

"Right, Right. I see what you're talking about. So, what do you want us to do when we get in there." JJ asked him. Jason sat back and closed his eyes. I looked at JJ and this nigga nods again.

Tank must have read my mind, cuz we both said fuck this. "Hey man, what the fuck was that?" I asked JJ cuz I knew damn well that Jason wasn't going to answer me. JJ looked at us both confused.

"Nigga, are you going to tell us are not." Tank said, getting aggravated.

"Man, y'all niggas sitting right here and didn't hear shit." JJ replied to us. Tank looked back at me, then at JJ. You can tell that he wanted to punch the shit out of him. "NOOOOO! We didn't understand that shit. Tell us nigga."

"J think something is up with this whole thing. Two hits with two misses. That shit doesn't sound right. And how many times did they request Jason to be at the table." JJ asked. That shit had us both thinking.

"Fa real, them niggas are too scared to have Jason sitting at the table." Tank said. I didn't have shit to say. I did what Jason did. I sat back, closed my eyes, and waited for this shit to unfold. Knowing Jason, he had several things up his sleeve.

THIRTY

JASON

I already knew that the members of this punk ass Stand was up to something. I told my brothers not to trust these niggas, and they did. One day, they gon' listen to me. I was sitting around the table listening to the lies about how "Dorian" escaped. I had eyes on his bitch ass son and he was more than fine. He was in Miami for Spring Break. So, whatever these niggas plans were after this was about to be canceled. None of them was going to make it home tonight.

I sat there, bored out of my fucking mind. I was ready for the blood, screams, and some torturing shit. I couldn't wait to get these bitches back at the warehouse. It was gonna keep me busy for a good week. Then on to my next kill. JJ and Jordan sat and waited for some type of signal from me.

"Jason," Derrick called.

I peered up at this hoe ass nigga that used to be my father's friend. It wasn't his fault that he became this way. They were all cool, until Jordan killed these people kids. Well, I killed them; Jordan ordered the shit. They were stupid to build back up our fortune, just to try and take it from us. Good luck, muthafuckers.

"Why don't you tell us why we are really here." I told them all.

Derrick looked at the other members. Stupid, dumb ass. This is why I don't sit at this fucking table. He looked back at us and smiled. "Can't get nothing past you, boy." He started laughing with the rest of the members. JJ, Jordan, and Tank just sat with blank expressions on their faces. They knew that I had them covered. Even then, fear is something that we don't show.

"I've been a man since I was twelve. Why don't you be one and stop playing these fucking games and tell us why we are really here. Last chance." I told him calmly. Their laughing stopped. And my smile grew.

Clap! Clap! Clap, was heard from the end of the table, where there were no doors.

"Sorry to interrupt yuh boys' scout meeting. Mi sure yuh cya hand out di merit badges lata." Some nigga said as he walked towards the table.

All of the older members of the Stand stood in surprise of our new guest. He was a tall, dark complexion man, with grey dreads hanging down his back. He looked young in the face, but you can tell that he was older. He was dressed in a fancy ass charcoal grey suit. Neither of us recognized him so, clearly, introductions were needed, or he was going to be another one of my victims. He looked at everyone at the table, but his eyes rested on mine. Something in his eyes was familiar.

"Callum. What are you doing here?" Sean asked with fear in his voice.

Callum's eyes looked at him in disgust. "Mi here fi personal mattas." He pulled up a chair and sat at the head of the table. JJ and Tank was looking at this nigga like some groupies. Jo was staring with the same blank expression as mine. Everyone knew that Callum was a cold ass assassin. There were stories about this nigga in everybody's hood. I started out using some of his techniques. But, I wasn't drooling over this nigga like some bitch.

"Mi ave hear dat di membas of dis boys club find out wah Jordan did fi yuh sons. An wa fi retaliate by a guh afta di pickney of di Davis crew, dat correct." He asked, while taking out his phone. Jordan looked at the members and waited for them to answer. "Please be quick bout it, mi ave otha shit to duh." Callum said calmly, but you can see that that nigga was holding on by a thread. Whatever these muthafuckers did must have been some bad shit to pull his ass out of retirement.

"You got damn right. These muthafuckers gotta suffer like we have been doing fa tha last past years." David Sr. spoke. You can tell that he'd been holding that shit in for a while. He was about to jump over the table and attack Jordan. Derrick held him back for whatever reason. He wasn't going to touch my fucking brother. On God, nigga. Callum laughed at David Sr. while he was tapping his phone.

"Suh yuh neva tink dat Senias death did enough." He looked up at David Sr. with pure fury. "My bredrin dying nuh enough huh." He said this with hurt and anger.

My father told us that him and Callum were close friends. We never knew how close, until he offered to pay for my father's funeral and opened up an account for my nephew. I didn't understand it until now. The expressions that he was showing was hard to fake. That was another reason why Lilly and JoJo got away from that hit. Callum had extra men on them.

"We didn't have anything to do with Senior murder, no parts of it. And you know that." Derrick spat at Callum.

"Dat a true, you neva." He said placing his phone away. He stood and glared at Derrick with dark, soulless eyes. "But yuh had everything to duh wid dis." Everybody could feel the coldness in his voice. I didn't know if him being close to my father had him here, but he had to understand that I wasn't going to let anything happen to my family. Especially after letting Pops down.

"Why is this any concern of yours?" Greg Sr. asked Callum. Callum looked at that nigga like he was an invalid. His eyes dropped back down, trying to keep his composure. He started breathing and knocking on the table.

"Di Davis pickney is mi business." He said with his eyes now opened on me. I didn't know what the fuck was going on with him staring at me and shit.

"Something to say," I asked Callum.

"Inna minute yougnsta, wait yuh tun." He told me. He looked back up at Derrick with darker eyes. "Mi tell yuh fuck boys, dat di Davis crew did nuh fi be touch. Mi guess mi warning neva mean shit to yuh."

"What do you know about pain, Callum? You have never gone through what we went through. So, you can't talk to me about shit, nigga. My son didn't deserve that shit from this punk ass boy. He trusted him, and that bitch played my son to get close to him. Only to kill him. And then I got to sit at this table with him, like everything is good. Fuck that. And if you down for that shit, fuck you too." Derrick said to Callum.

I knew that this shit was a bad idea from the start. JJ was feeling some type of way because Pops died. These old ass niggas were straight bugging right now. If they felt this way, why pretend? Here it is, this nigga thought that his connects were lined up to take us out. Bitch didn't have shit on us still.

"Fuck mi, hey." His knocks became harder and faster on the table. He was thinking of many ways to take Derrick out. I knew that because it was a look that I usually give when I was ready to kill. I was wondering what he was waiting on. Unless...this wasn't his kill. "Mi guess it nothing else for mi to sey......Shadow."

"Oh shit," Tank whispered.

Shadow came out of the shadows of the wall. He was dressed in all black with a hoodie. This nigga was tall as fuck. I couldn't tell you what this nigga looked like because his hood and dreads were covering his face. I knew he was about to wreck shit up.

"Gud, cuz mi did getting bore wid dis dialogue. Yuh did right before, wi duh ave betta shit to duh. Wah you tink Reap?" He said to the other side of the room.

Another nigga walked out of the shadows, on the other side of the room. JJ couldn't hold his composure this time. "Yo, it's about to get real in this bitch. Man, I need to IG this shit fa real." This nigga was pulling out his phone and all. Jordan slapped this nigga in the back of his head.

"Hold yo shit together nigga. The fuck wrong with you." Jordan said and snatched JJ phone away from him.

"Man, this is some epic, shit. Nobody ain't gon' believe this shit." He said to Jordan. We were all surprised to hear them niggas speak. Hell, if you saw them, that means that you only had a couple of minutes to live. So, to be in these niggas' presence was a fucking honor.

Reap walked all the way through with the hood over his head, with his dreads covering his face. He walked up to the table and stood next to Shadow, behind Callum. He shook his head and spoke.

"Mi tink wi should send dem to dem dead ones since dem cyaa live without dem." He spoke in a whisper but was heard through the room. The guards of the members started walking up closer to the table. But, the Elites weren't bothered by it. They were all hanging back for some reason.

"You still didn't tell us why you are here, Callum. There were many hits that you guys have done even if the job was restricted. The Davis crew is not exempt from this just because you and Senior was good friends." Derrick told him.

"Why him still chatting? Mi tink him did dun wen him say fuck yuh." Shadow said to Callum.

Callum pulled out his phone and started tapping on it again. He showed his phone to Shadow. Shadow shook his head at what he was seeing and smiled. He pulled out his phone and started recording what was going on.

"Mi tink yuh should gu ahead an kill dis one. There plenty more fi guh round." Reaper said.

Callum looked up at Derrick to speak, completely ignoring Reaper's suggestions. "Di pain yuh talk bout, mi nearly witness it di otha day. Di assassin yuh send at Davis pickney, came to mi yadd.

"They must have gotten the information wrong. We would have

never sent assassins to your home Callum." Greg said with so much fear in his voice. You can see that he was on the verge of breaking down. And these were the men that tried their hardest to take us down. Yeah right.

"Dem come fi di Davis Pickney. Dat a wah yuh pay dem fi, correct." Reap answered instead. Callum took a seat and waited for them to answer. They all nodded their head but was still confused. Shit, we all were. Why would the assassins be at Callum's house for my nephew and Lilly?

Shadow was losing his patience, right along with Callum. They all had rage in their eyes and they were all on me this time.

"Cuz, Jordan nuh di ongle one wid pickney.........Gage." He spoke. Now this was some epic shit. I knew it was over for these niggas. I truly was about to meet my idol. There were tapping sounds coming in from the shadow where Reap came from. We all were sitting on the edge of our seats. When the person came all the way in sight, carrying a head of a woman and a machete, my blood started boiling.

"Fuck! Are you serious right now, Nigga?" Jordan said, jumping up from his seat. Tank and Joseph were sitting there without breathing. I couldn't say anything myself. I didn't understand how this was even possible. Someone that fucked up, couldn't hide that type of crazy. I was seething with rage, bruh. I squeezed my fist so tightly that blood started dripping from my hand.

"Jordan. Tank. Joseph," Gage spoke in a colder voice than the others. I stood and watched Gage come closer to the table. Evil eyes were staring at me and I knew that my eyes were the same. Gage was wearing all black like Shadow and Reap, without the hoodie. The hair that was always in a ponytail, was wild and blonde. Gage tossed the head on the table. It rolled and stopped in front of Tank and me.

"Who the fuck was this?" JJ asked, while picking up the head. I didn't have to see it. I already knew who it was.

"Mya," I replied to him with my eyes still on Gage. Gage smiled up at me, and the shit was far from friendly.

"Jason." Gage greeted me. Jordan looked at me like, how was he still here. He made threats to have her missing and was still living to tell people about.

I didn't care. I let this type of craziness around my family and in my heart. I was ready for that dance that we were about to have before she walked out of my parents' house. I wasn't going to call her by the name she went by in the assassin world. I was going to call her the name that she gave me and my mother the first time we met. I gave her the same murderous smile and replied.

"Joel."

ACKNOWLEDGMENTS

Thanks to my family, publisher, and editor for the support. I am grateful and hope that I continue to make you all proud. To my only daughter, you inspire me sweetheart. You always remind me when things don't go right, go left.

CPSIA information can be obtained
at www.ICGtesting.com
Printed in the USA
LVOW13s1811280218
568199LV00016B/1064/P